MARIN COUNTRY DAY SCHOOL
LIBRARY
DONATED BY:
*Skidmore Family*
YEAR: *1984*

# Who Is Carrie?

# Who Is Carrie?

James Lincoln Collier · Christopher Collier

DELACORTE PRESS/NEW YORK

F
us

Published by
Delacorte Press
1 Dag Hammarskjold Plaza
New York, N.Y. 10017

Manufactured in the United States of America

First printing

LIBRARY OF CONGRESS CATALOGING IN PUBLICATION DATA

Collier, James Lincoln [date of birth].
Who is Carrie?

Summary: A young black girl living in New York City in
the late eighteenth century observes the historic events
taking place around her and at the same time solves the
mystery of her own identity.
1. United States—History—1789–1797—Juvenile fiction.
[1. United States—History—1789–1797—Fiction.
2. New York (N.Y.)—History—Fiction. 3. Slavery—
Fiction. 4. Afro-Americans—Fiction] I. Collier,
Christopher [date of birth]. II. Title.
PZ7.C678Wg 1984 [Fic]
ISBN 0-385-29295-3
Library of Congress Catalog Card Number: 83-23947

*For Harry and Jeanne*

# 1

I GOT DOWN to the harbor just as the bell in Trinity Church was ringing two o'clock. The streets was just as crowded as they could be, and down at the dock it was packed solid, everybody standing there looking out into the water, shouting and cheering and all of that.

I was late. I wished I'd got there sooner, but everybody at Mr. Fraunces' tavern was all in a sweat about General Washington coming to be inaugurated president, and they made me scrub over the kitchen twice, until everything gleamed, even though nobody said nothing about General Washington coming to the tavern, and even if he did come, he wasn't likely to go to the kitchen and fry himself some eggs. Presidents don't fry their own eggs; leastwise, not as I figured. We'd never had a president of the United States before, so I couldn't be sure. Maybe they did fry their own eggs, just to show they was plain folks and all.

But the cooks didn't care who was going to fry eggs, everything in the kitchen had to gleam like the moon, and so I sweat and moaned and told them I'd miss seeing the general land in the harbor; and they said I wasn't to go nowhere, I was to sit right there in the kitchen gleaming things until my arm fell off, and go on gleaming with the other arm after that. But of course *they* skidded off to see Washington themselves, like I knew they would, and as soon as they was out of sight I skidded off after them, going around by Greenwich Street instead of Broad Way so's nobody would spot me.

There wasn't nobody in the tavern when I left except the dogs, and they'd have gone, too, if they'd realized what was happening, but nobody told them. Oh, Mr. Fraunces, if he ever found out we'd all skidded off like that, he'd have had a fit. But I couldn't help myself—I just had to see General Washington. There wasn't any reason for seeing him. He was likely to be able to land himself without my help. It was just my dinged curiosity. I couldn't stand for anything to happen without me being in on it. It's why they called me Nosey.

It was sunny and beginning to get warm like it always does in late April in New York. It was a nice day to be out, and every dinged person in the city must have been on the streets. With all that crowd I couldn't see anything, anyway. I started to wriggle through, going sideways like a fish. They didn't like it none to see a scrawny little black girl wriggling around them

2

like that, pushing and shoving to the front, and they kept giving me looks. But I'd say, "I'm sorry, sir, I've got an important message for Mr. Fraunces." He kept the most famous tavern in New York—in the whole United States maybe, I reckoned—and people looked up to him. So I pushed on through, asking people if they'd seen Mr. Fraunces, and praying that they hadn't because if I ran into him he'd have a message for *me*, all right. And by and by I came out to the water front.

And there come General Washington. He was in a fancy barge with banners hanging from the side, being rowed by thirteen men in white suits. He was dressed in blue and buff and he was standing in the stern looking around and waving his hat when the people on the dock cheered, which was near constant. Coming beside him was a sloop with a choir of ladies on board it. They was singing something about, "Far be the din of arms, henceforth the olive's charms," which didn't make no sense to me. I couldn't see what olives had to do with it, unless maybe it was true that he cooked for himself and was going to make an olive pie to celebrate being elected president.

Other ships was in the harbor, too, and the cannons kept going off and the flags whipping around. Oh, there was such a hullabaloo you could hardly hear yourself cheer. It was just about the most exciting thing I ever went to, better than a horse race, and I cheered along with the rest of them, even though I couldn't hear my own voice for the cannonading. Finally the barge

3

pulled up to the dock. They'd got stairs there and carpet on the stairs, and a whole bunch of colonels and
congressmen and I didn't know what all, shined up like
kitchen pots, waiting for him. He climbed up the stairs
and shook hands around.

I wasn't more than thirty or forty feet from him. He
was very tall, over six feet I judged, and getting on for
sixty years old, and he had on about the most serious
look I'd ever seen on a man. You'd have thought that
being elected president, especially the first president of
a brand-new country that wasn't hardly a week old and
hadn't even got hair or teeth yet, he'd be smiling
around and congratulating himself on what a great man
he was. Most people would have.

If you elected an ordinary person president, why the
first thing they'd do is conclude they deserved it, and
grin around so's everybody could see how wonderful
they was. Horace would do it sure—he already thought
he was wonderful without being elected to anything. If
you elected one of the tavern dogs president, he'd think
he was wonderful and deserved it and get up on his
hind legs and grin, so's the people could see how great
he was. But General Washington, he just looked solemn
and shook everybody's hand. Maybe he was used to
being famous and it didn't mean anything to him anymore. Or maybe it was the olive pie that worried him.
It would have worried me, too.

The crowd made way for him and the colonels or
whatever they was lined up behind him, and they
began to march up the dock. And as the crowd thinned

out a little, I saw Mr. Fraunces. He was looking square at me. I didn't know if he recognized me from the distance, but I turned around quick as lightning and wriggled out of the crowd and shot for home.

It was a good thing I done it, too, because when I got back to the kitchen one of the dogs had elected himself butcher and was working over a chicken the cooks had got ready for dinner. About two minutes later the cooks come in, too. When they saw the chicken, they shouted at me for letting the dogs get it. I said it wasn't my fault, I'd just gone out to the pump for water, and if they'd been there it wouldn't have happened. They couldn't say nothing to that, so they just grumbled amongst themselves and told me to look sharper next time.

But I told Horace the truth about it. He come in from the market with a load of potatoes at suppertime. We took our plates and sat outside in the backyard by the pump where nobody'd bother us, and I told him. Horace was black like me and wouldn't tell on me to the cooks, who was white. Horace didn't call me Nosey, neither. I wouldn't let him, even if he was a grown man and I was supposed to do what he told me, being a girl. "I was standing close enough to touch him," I said, which would have been the truth if I'd had arms forty feet long.

He twisted himself around to look at me in that way he had, to see if I was making it up. Horace is mighty lanky, and he's always bending and unbending himself like a clasp knife. "That's the truth?"

5

"I swear it," I said, hoping I wouldn't get struck by a thunderbolt. "He even looked at me."

He bent and twisted for a minute, thinking about it and then he said, "Well, Carrie, I'd have gone down myself to see him, but I didn't want to bother him."

"Bother him? You wouldn't have bothered him none. There was thousands of people crowding around him already."

"Yes, I know that, Carrie. But if he'd seen me, he'd have felt obliged to come over and shake my hand. I didn't want to put him to the trouble."

I couldn't help laughing. "Horace, don't give me none of your stories."

"What do you mean, stories?" he said, like I'd hurt his feelings. "It ain't a story, it's the truth."

"All right, Horace," I said, "why would General Washington feel obliged to come over and shake your hand?"

"Why, I'm surprised you couldn't figure that out for yourself, Carrie."

"Figure out what?"

"Well, just look at it," he said, bending around to look at me square on. "You know about Dan's daddy fighting with General—I mean President Washington during the war."

I knew all about that. Dan Arabus told me about it a hundred times, how his daddy was in the fighting at Trenton and once he led General Washington's horse through a terrible rough stream and saved his life or some such, and Washington himself signed Dan's daddy's discharge papers. "I know about that, Horace," I said.

"Well, when the war was over they had a party for General—President Washington right at Mr. Fraunces' tavern—not this one, the one we had before over on Pearl Street."

I knew about that, too. When the war was over in 1783, General Washington had got all of his old officers together in the ballroom of the old tavern and made a speech and shook everybody's hand and kissed them and such and cried, too, they said. The cooks couldn't talk of nothing else for weeks afterward and they'd still start on it if you made a mistake and gave them a chance—how the first cook made a cake that Washington had held in his hand, and would have eaten, too, except that he was all choked up from saying farewell and wasn't hungry; and how the second cook had made the punch that General Washington drank so it was nearly the same as if she'd touched him herself; and how the third cook had washed the silver mug he'd drunk out of, which *was* the same as touching him, because some of his spit was bound to have got on it and naturally it come off on her when she'd washed the mug.

"Yes, Horace, I been bored by that story frequent enough," I said. "How does that make you and General Washington friends?"

"Why, it's clear as day, Carrie. General Washington

knew Dan's daddy and Dan's daddy was Willy's uncle and someday me and Willy are going to get married. It's as clear as day."

I laughed. "Horace, you beat anybody I ever knew."

His feelings was hurt. "Don't you get uppity with me, Carrie," he said.

"No, sah," I said. He twisted around to give me a look, but just then Mr. Fraunces come out through the kitchen door into the backyard. We jumped up. He stood there looking at us for a minute and I knew one of us was in trouble. I hoped it was Horace, which was uncharitable, but more healthy.

But it wasn't Horace. "What did you think of the spectacle this afternoon, Carrie?" Mr. Fraunces said, like he was making polite conversation.

I got hot and my supper began to set up like clay bricks in my stomach. "What spectacle, sir?"

"Why, General Washington's arrival, Carrie." He gave me a hard look. "You were there, weren't you? Or was it somebody who happened to look like you?"

Sweat began to run down my neck and the bricks began to knock around. "I reckon that was it, sir," I said. "You can't always recognize somebody from thirty or forty feet away."

He went on staring at me. "What put that particular distance in your mind?"

I'd put my foot in it. There was nothing I could say, so I just looked down at the ground and went on sweating and feeling the bricks in my stomach. He stared at me some more, and then he said, "Just see that you

8

don't run off like that again," and he went inside. I let out some air and my supper began to get limp again.

"I warned you about your blamed curiosity, Carrie," Horace said.

So had everybody else. But I was lucky: most any other master would have thrashed me for it.

# 2

Mr. Fraunces, he never thrashed me very much, even though I was curious—and uppity sometimes, too. He liked to think the best of people, he always said. He said that if you treated people well, they would treat you well, too. Sometimes when he said that it made me kind of ashamed of myself, for he *did* treat me well, and I was always skidding off some place, and lying about it afterward; although the way it seemed to me was that if you skidded off there wasn't no point in telling the truth about it afterward, it was just bound to hurt his feelings. But mostly I tried to do right.

Mr. Fraunces was all the family I had. I didn't know who my Ma was, nor my Pa, either. I could remember a long, long time ago, when I wasn't but a baby, being carried somewheres by a big black man. And I was crying, because he was taking me away from someplace, and I didn't want to go. Then he began singing to me in a low, slow voice. It made me feel safe, that low, slow voice did, and by and by I snuggled down in his arms and fell asleep. The next thing I remember after that was playing by the pump in the kitchen yard in back of Fraunces Tavern, and getting my dress all muddy from the water that had splashed on the ground, and one of the cooks smacking me on the behind.

Who was that big black man? Where was he taking me from? I didn't know. I'd asked Mr. Fraunces about it a good long while ago, and brought it up again from time to time. He only said he didn't know much about it, and anyway, the less I knew about it the better. The only thing he'd tell me was that my Pa died in the war. He said that was about all he knew about it. I had a feeling that he knew something more than that, though.

Oh, it was hard not knowing where I came from. I didn't even have no last name. I was a mystery to myself. Sometimes when I thought about it, it made me feel so sick and low I'd near bust out crying. If you didn't know who you was, you wasn't nobody. There ain't nothing much worse than being nobody.

But I had to make the best of it. Mr. Fraunces raised me as good as he could. Not himself of course: the cooks done the actual raising of me, or the upstairs maids, or whoever happened to have a hand free at the time to give me a smack. But Mr. Fraunces kept watch over me. He saw that I had doctoring when I needed it and every so often he'd call me down to his office and I'd stand there by his shiny desk on his beautiful rug and he'd ask me how I was, and did I go to church every Sunday and bathe regular and say my prayers, and didn't sass the cooks or have impure thoughts. Well, I answered yes I did, and no I didn't, and a good deal of it was even true. I bathed regular once a week, in summer leastwise, and I said my prayers, especially if I'd sassed one of the cooks and was headed for a whipping; and as for impure thoughts, when I found out what they was it was years too late to be sorry about it.

I couldn't complain much. Mr. Fraunces was kind and most of the time I forgot I was a slave and wasn't free to go off to some other place, like the cooks was. Of course the cooks was white and couldn't be slaves. But Horace, he was black like me and was free. He'd been born free, and even though he'd worked for Mr. Fraunces since he was a boy and never had worked no place else, he didn't have to stay there if he didn't want to. It wasn't fair; but there wasn't anything I could do about that, either.

Horace was my best friend at the tavern, but he wasn't my *best* best friend. That was Dan Arabus. Oh, Dan, he was wonderful. He'd come to the tavern a few years back and helped to take an important message down to Philadelphia and escaped out of a window and done all kinds of brave things, and Mr. Fraunces thought everything of him after that. But Dan wasn't

12

free, neither. He belonged to Captain Ivers, and worked on Captain Ivers' boat, the *Junius Brutus*, coming from Connecticut to New York or Philadelphia or even way down to the West Indies, to trade things.

When the ship was in New York, Dan would skid off to the tavern, and because of Mr. Fraunces thinking so high of him, he'd be allowed to take whatever he wanted to eat, and drink, too, and we'd go sit someplace and talk about things—about his plans for getting free, and his cousin Willy that Horace was in love with, and such. And that was the best of times for me, just sitting there talking to Dan. We was both slaves and maybe that was why we got on together, even if he was a few years older than me.

I figured Dan was likely to come along soon because of the inauguration next week: I figured Captain Ivers would want to be in on it. Everyone else was. All the beds in our tavern was taken, and the dining room was crowded, with people standing around waiting for a chance at a table, so's breakfast ran into midday dinner, and dinner ran into supper. The Spanish ambassador came in once wth some of his men, dressed so fancy it made you blink to look at them—scarlet coats with mother-of-pearl buttons, white silk waistcoats with flowers embroidered on them, silver buckles on their shoes. They was smoking Spanish cigars, long and thin as asparagus, that gave off such a wonderful smell I'd have gave a shilling just to try one, if I had a shilling.

And Mr. John Adams, who was to be vice-president,

he came in once with some people and ate his dinner. And Mr. Alexander Hamilton came in, who was some such thing I couldn't remember.

Horace got to serve Mr. Adams, and I thought I'd never hear the end of it—how Mr. Adams said Horace was the best waiter he'd ever had, and smart, and could have been a top man at anything he tried, if he wasn't black.

So everybody came to the tavern, but Dan. Five days of it, and still he didn't come, and he didn't come, and I began to worry. Whenever I got the chance, I'd skid out into the backyard and look to see if he was coming up the alley alongside the tavern. But he never was, and finally the cooks began to tell me to stop worrying about Dan and keep my mind on my business, he'd come when he come and anyway, Dan was probably sick or drowned or fell in love with some pretty girl up in Connecticut and was going to marry her.

"He wouldn't fall in love with nobody," I told them.

"He wouldn't fall in love with no sassy scullery maid, that's certain."

It made me blush when they said that, and I resolved I wouldn't let anyone see me skidding out to look for Dan anymore, but I couldn't help myself and would forget and they would start it again about Dan being in love, or in jail for stealing. I decided to put Dan out of my mind the best I could. It wasn't doing me no good to dwell on him.

Besides, the inauguration was only two days away. I

14

was curious as could be about it. We'd had inaugurations before, when they'd put in a new governor and such, but this one was a president of a brand-new country. How was I going to get out? Mr. Fraunces wasn't of no mind to let me go, seeing as how I'd skidded off to watch General Washington land in his barge, and he was sure to thrash me this time if he caught me. Besides, the cooks, they all wanted to go themselves, and was certain to make me stay behind to see the dogs didn't elect themselves butcher to a chicken again. So I just didn't see how I was going to do it.

The day come. Everybody knew it, but still at sunrise they fired off a cannon down at the Battery just in case anybody missed out on the news. Then at nine o'clock all the church bells around the city began banging away, and most near everybody went off to a special service to pray for General Washington and the new government. Of course, I didn't go. The cooks, they wasn't so particular as Mr. Fraunces about me going to church, not when there was work to do; nor having impure thoughts, either, come to think of it, judging from the amount of cursing that got done around the kitchen.

So me and the cooks stayed and got breakfast ready for them all when they came back; and after that we cleaned up, and set up for dinner, which was likely to go on all afternoon with them all celebrating the new government and hollering and making toasts and drinking such a quantity of rum punch as would turn them all red in the face. And then when we got the dining room ready, the cooks set me down behind a pile of potatoes so high I couldn't hardly see over it, all needing to be peeled whether they wanted it or not.

And I was setting there peeling when away in the distance there came the sound of fifes and drums, and we knew the parade had started. Oh, I was downhearted. I wanted to be in on it in the worst way. Then one of the stable boys sent himself on an errand to get some oats, and come back and said that the parade was coming down Broad Street and it was the grandest thing he'd ever seen.

It made me cross and fretful. It wasn't fair that everybody else was out watching the parade and I daren't leave. Then, after a bit, the first cook said she'd just remembered it was her auntie's birthday, and she ought to stop around with a bit of cake to cheer her up, as she wasn't long for this world.

"I thought she passed on last year," the second cook said, mighty sharp.

"That was my other old auntie," the first cook said. So she wrapped up a chunk of cake in a piece of cloth and went off. And she hadn't been gone for more than three minutes when the second cook said she was worried about her old auntie, too—she couldn't remember exactly when her birthday was, but it was around this time and it would hurt the old dear something awful if she missed it. So she wrapped up a piece of cake and went off, too. Well, the third cook stood it for about three minutes more. Then she said she didn't have no dear old auntie, but she was dinged if she was going to stay around the kitchen while the others was off at the parade; nor miss out on the cake, neither. So she took a piece of cake and told me she'd be back in ten minutes and if I didn't have the potatoes peeled when she got back she'd peel me with a hickory switch.

I could hear the fifes whistling and the drums thrumming off in the distance. Oh, I was about ready to bust. I got up and peeked out into the dining room, where I wasn't allowed except to clean the pewter candle sconces when nobody was around. There wasn't nobody there. The whole tavern was dead silent except for the kitchen dogs scratching outside somewheres and the fifes whistling and the drums thrumming. I couldn't stand it no more and I just turned and run out of there, figuring if I stayed for five minutes, just long enough to have one little peek at the parade, my curiosity would be satisfied and I'd be comfortable with myself and wouldn't mind peeling them potatoes.

I ran down the alley beside the tavern into Cortlandt Street and across Broad Way over to Maiden Lane. Most days there would have been lots of people going along Broad Way and carts trundling along, but today there wasn't nobody there—they was all at the parade. I got along a little, when I realized that the fifes and drums wasn't coming from Queen Street no more; they was coming from a little further downtown, and I realized that the parade must have already got to City Hall. I stopped running. It made me sick to think I'd missed seeing George Washington parade by. There'd be a huge mob down there, and it would take too much time to push my way through to try to see him. It was too risky.

But then I thought, if I ran down there quick I could at least see what the crowd looked like and maybe that would satisfy me a little. So I ran along Maiden Lane and down Nassau Street towards Wall. As I got closer the crowd got thicker and thicker until it was packed so tight I could hardly wriggle through. I knew I ought to stop and go back. It was likely that the cooks was headed back already. But I kept on pushing forward, not able to see anything but skirts and belts and trousers and overhead just a scratch of blue sky, until I banged smack into a lamp post. I looked up. There was a couple of boys up there, younger than me. So I grabbed ahold of the post, shinnied up it five feet, and clung there, looking out over the crowd.

Right ahead of me was City Hall, a mighty big stone building with windows shining in the sun, and a flagpole on top with no flag up it. There was a little balcony jutting out from the second floor over the door. They'd set up a table there and a couple of chairs. There was a red velvet cloth on the table; and on the cloth a crimson velvet cushion; and on the cushion a big book which I reckoned was a Bible.

Nobody was on the balcony, and the crowd just watched and waited. Then suddenly a bunch of men came out onto it. One of them was John Adams, and another one was Governor Clinton, who I seen plenty of times at the tavern, and another was Mr. Livingston, who was some big muckety-muck. And of course General Washington. I didn't know who the rest were. Well, the crowd let out a shout, and then they fell dead silent. Nobody even whispered or stirred, but stood stock-still, watching.

General Washington come to the front of the balcony, laid his hand on his heart, bowed around to everybody a few times, and went and sat down in a chair near to the table with the Bible on it. The crowd went on standing ever so quiet. Finally, Washington stood up and laid his hand on the Bible. Mr. Livingston stood opposite and read out the oath, which was all big words and got past me without leaving no stain on my brain. General Washington put his hand on the Bible and said it all back. When he was done he bent down and kissed the Bible.

Someone shouted, "Long live George Washington." A flag shot up the flagpole on top of the building. The church bells all around the city began to clang, the cannons down at the Battery began to bang, the people began to shout and fling their hats up in the air, which wasn't sensible as they'd never find them again. A chill went up my back and across my head.

I slid down the lamp post, wriggled through the crowd, and raced back up Nassau Street, doing enough praying as would satisfy Mr. Fraunces for a month. And I had just swung into Cortlandt Street and was about a half minute from the tavern, when I felt a hand clap over my eyes and another over my mouth. Someone had caught me.

19

# 3

HE WAS BIG AND he was strong. He'd got his hands, smelling like tar, all over my face, and his elbows clenched against my sides to pin my arms tight. But my legs was free and I began kicking back behind me as hard as I could, trying to get him in the shins if I could; and about the third kick I caught hold of him good with my heel and he cursed. The hands across my mouth was tight and it hurt. I opened my mouth and snapped it closed, and I felt my teeth go into his flesh. He cursed again and snatched his hand off my eyes and gave me a terrible clout alongside my head that made me dizzy. Then he covered my eyes again.

But in that couple of seconds when my eyes was uncovered I saw Dan standing by the alley that led around back of the tavern. "Dan," I screamed and the hand clapped back over my mouth. This time he jammed a cloth in my mouth and the next minute flung a bag over my head that come all the way down to my waist. He whipped a rope around the bag and pulled it tight so my arms couldn't move. I was trussed up like a pig ready for market. I felt myself lifted up and the next thing I knew I was flung over his shoulder and he was trotting off down the street.

The cloth in my mouth was making me choke and gag, and the bag itched my face and made it hard to breathe. I began shoving at the rag with my tongue and in a bit I got it out of my mouth, and after that I could breathe easier. I could shout, too, but I didn't dare, for he'd know that I'd got the rag out and shove it back in again. All I could do was pray that Dan had seen me and would find a way to save me.

Oh, I was scared, and shaking and sick inside, so scared I could hardly think. But I knew what it was: a kidnapper. There was plenty of them around New York, and black folks had to be mighty careful about them for they was always looking to kidnap some black person and sell them off to the South, where they'd work in the fields from sunup until sundown, hoeing tobacco or cutting sugarcane until they was wore out. Niggers was worth a lot of money. Dan figured I was worth fifty pounds in the West Indies, more in Virginia, which was more money than I was likely to see as long as I lived. And that was where I was headed. But all I

21

could do was lie there over the kidnapper's shoulder, shaking and trembling, so scared and sick I couldn't cry.

He carried me along for a ways, and by and by he stopped. I heard a key clink and a door squeak open, and then I was thrown down like a sack of corn, knocking the wind out of me and scraping my back. The door squeaked closed and the key clinked in the lock.

For a minute I lay there, listening. I could hear a kind of muffled sound of carts rumbling along the cobblestones, and the squeaking of a pulley, and I could smell tar and the sea, so I knew I was down by the docks. That shook me even worse, for that meant they was planning to ship me off to the West Indies, where I wouldn't do nothing but cut sugarcane in the baking heat and dust for the rest of my life. In the West Indies there wouldn't be no chance of escaping, and I'd never get back home, and never see nobody again.

The reason why I knew all about kidnappers and being shipped off to the West Indies and such was because it almost happened to Dan's cousin Willy, the one that Horace was in love with. Willy's Ma had got terrible sick during the Revolution, and had gone to live with Captain Ivers, who was master of Dan and his mother. They was kin to Willy, which is why Willy went there. But Willy's Ma had died because Captain Ivers wouldn't buy her no medicine, and Willy had got into a terrible fight with Captain Ivers and had run off, and ended up down at the tavern working for Mr. Fraunces, the same as me. But Captain Ivers, he put it out everywhere that Willy was his slave. He didn't have no proof of it—no bill of sale or nothing. But he said it, anyway. The problem was that Willy didn't have no proof that she was free, either. Her Pa had got killed in the war, and her Ma had died up there at Captain Ivers' place. Her Pa had had papers saying he was free back up in Connecticut at Groton where they lived before the Revolution, somewheres up in the old shack where they used to live. But that was a long time ago and Willy figured the papers was long gone, and the shack as like as not, too.

She was supposed to get some papers from a judge up in Connecticut once, but she'd run off to New York and somehow the papers never come. Without papers nobody was going to believe her against Captain Ivers. He was white and she was black, and nothing but a girl, too; nobody was going to believe her. Captain Ivers knew that as well as Willy did. He was bound and determined to catch her. And once when she was out front of the tavern washing down the steps, two men come and made a snatch at her and tried to heave her into a wagon, but she got away. She knew that if Captain Ivers caught her she would be a slave. She told me, "Nosey, I might just as well be a slave. I got to go somewhere else where Ivers can't find me." So she went off to Philadelphia. It was mighty sad for her and Horace.

Oh, they wrote letters, but that wasn't the same. Horace, he always claimed to be a prince at writing, but from watching the way he jabbed the pen around, poking holes in the paper and blotching it, I could tell he wasn't no great shakes at it. And Willy, she was just teaching herself to read and write and wasn't no great shakes at it, either. So they was pretty lonely for each other. Anyway, that's how I come to know what the kidnappers was up to. And knowin what I was in for made it worse than not knowin.

Anyway, I was in worse trouble myself now. I listened some more, real careful. I didn't hear sounds of breathing or anybody moving around, and I figured I was alone, wherever I was. I kneeled up and then I stood, easing up carefully in case I was in a shed with a low ceiling. But I wasn't. I could stand straight. Then I began to shuffle slowly around, feeling with my hands and feet for things. In a moment I bumped into something. I felt it with my legs. It seemed like a box or a chest of some kind. I felt around some more and bumped into another chest, and then a bag of something. I knew I was in the storehouse, filled with things waiting to be loaded onto some ship. I was just cargo like the boxes and bags.

The rope going around me was pretty tight, and my arms was beginning to feel numb and my fingers were getting stiff. My head was beginning to hurt where the kidnapper had clouted me, too. The first thing I had to do was get the bag off my head so I could see around a little, and then after that maybe I could spot something to cut the rope with.

There was bound to be a loose nail, or a rough edge of a hasp or something on one of the chests, that I could

24

rip the bag with. I sat down on one of them, and slid my bottom along real easy this way and that, and in a minute I felt something sharp—a nail that wasn't pounded all the way in, I figured, or maybe part of a hinge or something. I got off the chest and knelt down over it. Then going as careful as I could, so as not to poke my eye out, I bent my head over it until I could feel the sharp thing touching my chest. I hooked the cloth of the bag into it, and jerked. There was a little ripping sound. I hooked the sharp thing into the rip I'd made, and gave it a hard, steady pull. The bag began to tear open, and in a minute I'd made a nice big rip in it and could see out.

It was dark in there, and gloomy, and only a couple of small windows on either side of the door let in a little light. It was a storehouse, just like I figured, with chests and barrels and sacks heaped up all around, and a dirt floor. There was dust all over everything. It made the cobwebs thick as strings hanging down from the beams everywhere. The windows hadn't been washed for years, neither.

I hobbled over to the door, and took a look out of one of the windows, keeping back a little so's nobody could see me from the outside. I was facing a dock. I could see ships tied up, with their long bowsprits sticking out over the street, and bales and boxes and things stacked up everywhere along the cobblestones that had just been unloaded or was waiting to be loaded on.

Where was the kidnapper? I looked around the street. Two or three men was lounging around the dock

25

—a couple of them sitting on a stack of boxes, one hunkered down mending a rope, another one leaning on the corner of a building smoking a pipe. I had no way of knowing if they was just sailors, or the kidnapper keeping an eye out so I couldn't escape.

I hobbled back away from the window so as to be out of sight, and stood there thinking. My arms was hurting worse and my fingers getting number, and I was still good and scared, but being able to see helped a little: at least I knew what was going on around me. But what should I do? I figured I could break out one of the windows and squeeze through. Once I was out it wouldn't be no trouble getting away, even though my arms was tied down.

The big problem was whether one of them men outside was the kidnapper. If it was, I'd be better off waiting until dark, when maybe he'd go off to get his supper, or would get sleepy, or would figure I wasn't able to find a way to escape. But if I waited too long they might load me on the ship and lock me in the hold and once I was on board there wasn't no way I could escape short of throwing myself into the water and drowning.

No, it didn't make no sense to wait. So I hobbled back over to the window, feeling mighty trembly. I took a deep breath to calm myself down. Then I leaned my shoulders, which was pretty well protected by the bag, against the window, just pushing steady, and in a minute it cracked and fell to pieces. I leaped back and looked out, and my heart sank. The man who had been leaning on the corner of the building smoking shoved the pipe into his coat pocket and came running toward me. I pushed my face down by the broken window and began to shout, "Help, help, help," as loud as I could. Some of the people around stopped what they were doing, and looked up. "Help," I shouted. But the kidnapper was at the door, clinking his key. I hobbled over behind the door. It swung open and the kidnapper ran in. I was out from behind the door and around it like a shot and into the street.

But it was useless, trussed up the way I was. He was on me in two steps, grabbed hold of the bag and started to pull me back toward the storehouse. And that was when I seen Dan and Mr. Fraunces trotting along the street.

"Dan," I shouted and the next thing I knew Mr. Fraunces had the kidnapper by the arm and was shaking him. Dan grabbed him by the other arm and they shoved him up against the side of the little low warehouse where they had captured me.

"Let go of me," the kidnapper shouted.

"Oh, no," Mr. Fraunces said. "You're going straight down to the jail."

That worried the kidnapper some. He gave Mr. Fraunces a look, and then me, and he spit onto the cobblestones and looked back at Mr. Fraunces. "Let go of me," he growled. "You ain't got no right to hold me." He tried to jerk loose, but Mr. Fraunces banged his shoulder hard onto the kidnapper, and slammed him back against the wall.

27

It hurt him, and he winced. Then he said, "You ain't got no right to hold me. That little nigger girl don't belong to you."

Mr. Fraunces gave a kind of a jump. He stared at the kidnapper hard. "Who told you that?" he said.

The kidnapper looked away. "None of your business how I know."

Mr. Fraunces gave the kidnapper a shake by the arm. "I'll make it my business," he said in a rough voice.

"I seen legal papers," the kidnapper said. "You ain't her rightful owner."

Well, it was all pretty surprising to me, and mystifying, too. But maybe the kidnapper was lying.

Mr. Fraunces gave him another shake. "Who hired you?" he shouted.

The kidnapper pulled himself up straight and looked at Mr. Fraunces direct, like he knew he had the upper hand. "I ain't going to tell you," he said. "And if you take me into court, I'll prove that you ain't her rightful owner."

Mr. Fraunces stood there holding onto the kidnapper, his eyes narrowed, thinking. Dan stared at him, and me, and the kidnapper, too. Then Mr. Fraunces said quietly, "Let him go, Dan."

They backed off from the kidnapper and he slipped away from the wall. Mr. Fraunces raised his arm and pointed his finger into the kidnapper's face. "But if I see you anywhere near my tavern again I'll have the stable-boys beat you within an inch of your life," he shouted. "Is that clear?"

The kidnapper gave Mr. Fraunces a quick look, spit on the cobblestones, and strolled off down the street, lighting up his pipe as he went.

Well, I was confused all right. It seemed clear enough that the kidnapper wasn't lying. I looked up at Mr. Fraunces. "Sir, who do I belong to, then?"

He gave me a hard look. "As far as you're concerned, you belong to me. Just leave it at that."

"Please, sir, it ain't fair. It's mighty hard not knowing who you are." I went on looking up at him. "Please, sir."

He shook his head. "I didn't want any of this to get out. It's bad."

"Please, sir."

He thought some more, and then said, "I guess they've found out some of it," he said sort of to himself. "I suppose I might as well tell you this much anyway. The man who brought you to the tavern was Jack Arabus."

"Dan's daddy?" I looked at Dan and Dan looked at me. "Why didn't you tell me, Dan?"

He shook his head. "I didn't know anything about it until this minute."

"Sir," I said—

He held up his hand. "I'm sorry this much has gotten out. That's all I'm going to say about it. We'll drop it there." He gave me a serious look. "But from now on keep a sharp eye out for yourself, Carrie."

And I was mighty sure I would.

DAN STAYED at the tavern for a while that evening. There was parties everywhere at night, and fireworks, and people putting up pictures of Washington in front of their houses, and lighting candles in the windows, so that the whole city was shining with light. Dan said Captain Ivers was going around seeing it all so he didn't have to be in any rush to get back to the *Junius Brutus.*

Dan figured he'd be coming down to New York pretty frequent from now on. Now that we was one country, and had a president, there was going to be good business and prosperity. Least that was what Captain Ivers was saying. New York was bound to grow and the people would need most everything you could think of—hogs and beef and shingles and staves, and I don't know what all. Captain Ivers, he didn't care what he sold, so long as there was money in it, Dan said. He'd buy cows from farmers in Connecticut, or molasses in 'Stacia in the West Indies, or tobacco in Virginia, or whatever, and bring it back to New York and sell it there at a profit. Oh, Dan had been everywhere, and there was nothing I liked better than to hear him tell about it.

So that night, once we got supper served and the kitchen cleaned up, and the men in the dining room was eating nuts and fruit and drinking a considerable quantity of wine and Madeira and rum punch, me and Dan sat out back by the pump, eating up the cake that was left after the cooks chopped off most of it for their old aunties.

We talked about Dan's daddy bringing me to the tavern. "It sure surprised me," I said.

"It surprised me, too," he said.

"You don't know nothing about it, Dan?"

"Not a drop. My daddy never said anything to me about it. I reckon he might have sometime, if he wasn't drowned first."

I thought about it. "Dan, I'll bet you anything my daddy knew your daddy."

"Why?"

"My daddy was killed in the war. Most likely he was a friend to your daddy. Most likely they was soldiers together. And my daddy, he got killed and he told your daddy I was lying all by myself in his shack back home. And as he lay there dying with the blood seeping out of

31

him, he made your daddy promise to take care of me. So your daddy done that, and brought me to the tavern because he couldn't have no baby in the army." It made me feel good to think that Dan's daddy and my daddy was friends.

Dan give a laugh. "That sounds like a story out of a book," Dan said.

I was hurt. I liked thinking that our daddies was friends. "You know I can't read no book."

"Well, anyway, there was lots of men killed in the war. Willy's father was killed in the Battle of Groton. It doesn't mean our daddies were friends, just because your daddy was a soldier, too."

"Then how did your daddy get ahold of me, Dan?"

"I don't reckon anybody will ever know that, Carrie," he said. "I just wished my daddy hadn't got himself drowned. By now he'd have saved up enough money to buy me and Ma free." Dan was always talking about being free.

"It's in front of me all the time, Carrie," he said. "Sometimes when I'm busy steering the ship or trimming sails, it goes off my mind for a while, but as soon as I ain't busy anymore it slips right back again. I can't help it. It doesn't do any good to worry about it day in and day out, but I get reminded of it. There's hardly anything that doesn't remind me of it. If I see a sign up hiring sailors onto a ship for thirty shillings a month, I can't take the job, because I got to work for Captain Ivers for nothing. Or if I see a pretty girl and want to marry her, why I couldn't do that, either, because I ain't got any place to keep a girl, and what girl wants to go with a slave that hasn't any prospects?"

I said, "If she was a slave herself, she might."

"Well, yes, but there's the other side to it," he said. "Suppose I was to get married to some girl who was a slave. Then suppose the government pays off everybody's notes, and I get enough money to buy me and Ma free. What would happen to my wife? I wouldn't be able to go anywhere anyways, because she'd be stuck."

"You could buy her free, too."

He shook his head, and looked grim. "It'll be plain luck if the notes will be worth enough to buy two people free, much less three. It'll be plain luck if they'll be worth anything at all."

Dan's notes was pretty confusing, and as frequent as he'd explained it to me, I never did understand the ins and outs of it all. What happened was Dan's father, who was Jack Arabus, fought in the Revolution right next to General Washington. He got free for fighting and a whole lot of money, too. Only it wasn't real money. It was just pieces of paper called notes that said the government owed you some money.

Well, of course Dan's daddy got drowned, and after that the notes belonged to Dan. Captain Ivers, he tried to get them away from Dan, but Dan got them back, and for safekeeping give them to Dr. William Samuel Johnson, who was rich and famous and lived near Dan's Ma. Johnson wasn't in Connecticut no more, he was president of Columbia College in New York City, not far from our tavern. He'd got Dan's notes there.

33

The thing was, nobody knew if the notes would be worth real money. It was up to the government to decide if they would pay them off or not. And on top of it, the states had put out their own notes, too, which people had taken instead of real money, and nobody knew if they'd be worth anything, either.

So naturally, while everybody was waiting to see if the states could get together and make themselves into one big country, some people was going around buying other people's notes for a cheap price. Say, if your notes was worth a hundred dollars, somebody might give you a dollar, or ten dollars or something for them on the gamble that the states would be able to get themselves together. And finally they did get themselves together and made the United States of America; and people who owned these notes was mighty cheered up, because they figured that the government would pay them off. Maybe they wouldn't pay them off a hundred percent, but they might declare that your hundred-dollar note was worth fifty dollars or some such.

But then it come out that *maybe* the government would pay off the notes and *maybe* they wouldn't. And it also come out that *maybe* they would pay off the states' notes for them, too, and *maybe* they wouldn't. The whole thing was as full of maybes as a bushel of potatoes, and it was making people like Dan, who'd got notes, just wild crazy. One day a rumor would go around that the congress was going to vote to pay the notes off, and the price of them would go up; and then the next day a contrary rumor would go around, and the price would go down. And nobody knew what to do.

And for Dan it wasn't just the money. It was freedom, because if they paid off the notes a hundred percent, he'd have six hundred dollars, and maybe more, which would be enough to buy his freedom, and his Ma's, too. But if they decided the other way, the notes wouldn't be worth nothing, and Dan and his Ma would have to stay slaves and work for Captain Ivers the rest of their lives.

"What are they worth now, Dan?" I said.

"Right now about half," Dan said. "People are buying them for half, because now that there's a government and a president and all, they figure there's a good chance that Congress will vote to pay them off. My notes is worth three hundred dollars, I reckon."

"That's a powerful lot of money," I said. "I'd sell them. I wouldn't risk waiting around. I'd sell them quick."

"It's a powerful lot," he said, "but it ain't enough to buy both me and Ma off. Captain Ivers, he said, if I gave him the notes he'd set me free, but that would leave Ma stuck."

"You know what I'd do," I said. "I'd grab the money and buy myself free and then work and save up money until I had enough to get my Ma free."

Dan shook his head. "I thought about that. I reckoned it up. It would take me near ten years to save up three hundred dollars. That's a powerful lot of money for anyone to save, and worse for a black man who don't get paid the same as whites."

That's how smart Dan was. I wouldn't have thought to reckon it up, even if I could have. I'd have just started saving and wouldn't realize how long it would take until years later. But Dan, he ciphered it out. Oh, he was smart. "What are you going to do?"

"Chance it," he said. "Chance it that the new government will pay off the notes a hundred percent."

And what about me? I thought. Horace was free and Willy was free and Dan could get himself free anytime he wanted to, and even his Ma, who I didn't even know, might get free. And I didn't have no chance of it. It wasn't fair. Why was Dan so all-fired set on getting his Ma free? She was old, and might die, and then the money would be gone and he wouldn't have his Ma, neither. I knew I shouldn't ought to be thinking like that. It was bad to think evil of other people, and wish they would die. But I couldn't help myself.

Of course, there was one other thing: running away. It wasn't something that black folks talked about a whole lot. You didn't want nobody putting it around that you was even talking about running away, because if your master found out, he was likely to sell you off like that, so's he'd get something back on you. But the idea was always there in my mind, and I reckoned it was in the minds of most slaves, too. I never thought about it serious, though. Mr. Fraunces had raised me up, and treated me like I was kin, and I wouldn't like to do nothing to hurt him. Besides, where would I run off to? But the idea was always in mind. I didn't want to say anything to Dan, though. So I said, "What would you do if you was free, Dan?"

"Save up and buy a fishing dory, like my Pa. I'd fish out on Long Island Sound, and sell fish in New Haven."

That worried me. "You wouldn't come down to New York no more?"

"Well I might," he said. "I don't know. Ma, she wouldn't want to leave Connecticut. I'd probably stay up there."

Oh, it was worrisome. I could see that Dan getting free wasn't going to do me no good no way you looked at it, unless I got myself free, too. And I didn't see how I was going to do that. Thinking about it, I began to feel low and miserable. There was hope for everybody else, but there wasn't no hope for me.

# 5

ONE OF THE JOBS I done around there was carrying out dinners for them as was too lazy to come to the tavern —cooked lobsters, or oysters, or beef a la mode, which was put up in a sauce. They'd send over a message they wanted such and such for dinner and the cooks would get it ready, and I'd cart it over in a bucket as fast as I could so it wouldn't cool down. The bucket was heavy and bumped against my legs as I trotted along with it, but I didn't mind, because it gave me a chance to get out and have a look around.

I'd wonder about the people I saw coming along—what they was thinking, and what kind of a house they had, and whether they was happy or had some sorrow in their lives and was sad. Or I'd see a dead horse lying in the streets, with his legs sticking out, looking just like he was alive and would get up any minute; and I'd wonder what it was like to be dead and not feeling nothing at all.

Or I'd see the birds twittering around in the trees, and I'd wonder what it would be like to be able to fly away to wherever you wanted—up on top of a roof or into a church steeple, or just go away, way up and look down. That's what I'd do if I could fly—go way, way up and look down, and see the whole of New York City all at once, the buildings so tiny and the people no bigger than cockroaches. I'd give anything to have wings. I'd fly away and never be a slave no more. If I had wings I wouldn't be able to pick up a bucket of oysters, or pump water, or peel potatoes, anyway.

A couple of days after the inauguration, one of the professors at Columbia College ordered up some beef a la mode. They was always ordering food, them professors—they was too smart to cook for themselves. Off I went, and when I come back I saw Mr. Fraunces standing in front of the tavern talking to a gentleman. He was younger than Mr. Fraunces and he was dressed in a blue coat and yellow waistcoat and had silver buckles on his shoes. He looked mighty rich. They was talking serious, and naturally I was curious. But I couldn't just stand there and listen—if Mr. Fraunces wanted an audience he would let me know. So I went into the alley that ran along side the tavern, and when I was out of sight of them I stopped and cocked my head.

"This is a serious proposal, Mr. Lear?" I heard Mr. Fraunces say.

"President Washington was quite definite about it."

"I consider it a great honor," Mr. Fraunces said.

"The President feels you are equal to it."

"I would hope to be worthy. I would hope to set the best table in the United States."

Just then one of the cooks come around the corner. Quick as I could I knelt down, took off my shoe, and gave it a shake, like I got a stone in it. "Where've you been so long, Nosey?" she said.

"You ain't supposed to call me Nosey," I said.

"Don't you get sassy with me, you little pickaninny," she said. She come down the alley and snatched at my ear to give it a twist, but I ducked around her and went into the kitchen, where there was a stack of potatoes near as high as I was waiting for me and them no more glad to see me than I was them. And I was peeling away at them, thinking that I didn't so much mind that God made potatoes—they was mighty good roasted, but why did he have to put their skins on so tight?—when the third cook came in all flushed and bustling with something to tell. "You ain't going to believe this, everybody," she said. "Mr. Fraunces, he's going to work for President Washington."

Well, that stopped the whole kitchen dead in its tracks. We all gathered around and she stood there saying, "Don't all holler; how can I tell you about it if you're all asking questions at once?" She didn't have the chance to be the center of things too often, and I could see she was going to stretch it out if she could. But the others kept jabbering at her and she had to tell it. George Washington, he'd asked Mr. Fraunces to be his

40

steward, which was to be in charge of the kitchen and the cooks and the waiters and other help. And Mr. Fraunces was going to take the job. More than that, he was going to take some of the help from the tavern along with him to the President's house.

"Oh, lands," the third cook said. "Imagine cooking at the President's house, with all them generals and congressmen and admirals and maybe kings from Europe, too, sitting around. It'd scare me so I'd drop."

The second cook gave her a sharp look. "It ain't nothing you have to worry about," she said. "Mr. Fraunces ain't likely to take no cook who burns water boiling eggs." It was true—the day before the third cook had set a pot of eggs on the fire and let the water boil away and cooked the eggs until they was black.

"I ain't the only one who burned things around here," the third cook shot back. That was true, too—the second cook got drunk once on a Sunday when everybody was off to church and fell asleep and burned a whole roast beef.

"Be quiet, the two of you," the first cook said. "It beats all how either of you, as can hardly make a pot of tea without spilling something or burning something or dropping something in the fire, could have the presumption to think Mr. Fraunces would consider taking either of you anywheres near the President's house, much less inside of it. Mr. Fraunces, he'll know who to take to cook for President Washington," meaning she knew he ought to take her even if the rest of them didn't.

41

Well, it was exciting to think about working for the President with all those famous men swimming around and deciding how to run the country. But I knew there wasn't no point in my thinking about it much, because I wouldn't be part of the excitement. I reckoned Mr. Fraunces would take the first cook, no matter if she put on airs because she was first cook. And I reckoned he might take one of the other cooks, too, and some of the waiters. He might take Horace.

But he couldn't take everybody, he had to leave somebody to work at the tavern. And I was pretty confident that he wasn't likely to take over to the President's house a sassy black kitchen maid who was always skidding off someplace and putting her nose in where it didn't belong. It made me wish I'd behaved better. It made me wish I'd been good and worked hard and didn't sass nobody and said my prayers and not had impure thoughts, even if I didn't know what they was until it was too late. Maybe if I'd done all that Mr. Fraunces would have thought particular high of me, the way he thought high of Dan for being brave and such; and if he'd thought high of me why maybe he'd have said to himself, "Carrie is just so wonderful at working and not having impure thoughts, I believe I'll take her with me to the President's house." But it was too late for that.

So feeling sort of down I went back to the potatoes and listened to the cooks chatter on about what it would be like to work for George Washington, and how there would be mountains of silver plate gleaming everywhere and fine china come from England and France with pictures painted on them, and heaps of food with no stinting on cream and butter and spices— just fling in as much as you wanted and not think twice about it.

So that gave me another thing to keep out of my mind, and I closed my ears off to it and thought about Dan's Ma dying suddenly before he could buy her off and he bought me off instead and maybe we set up in some business together—a store, maybe. And because he was so smart we'd make a lot of money and I'd help run the store, and be good for a change and not go skidding off, and—well, things like that. Thinking about that, I hardly noticed the potatoes.

And I was sitting there like that dreaming and peeling potatoes when suddenly I realized that I was hearing somebody shouting out in the dining room. I come up out of my daydream, and listened, and the cooks stopped what they was doing and listened, too.

It was two men, and in a minute I realized one of them was Mr. Fraunces, arguing with somebody. "I want you out of my place," he said in a loud voice.

"This is a public tavern," the other voice said. "By law I can stay here as long as I'm not disturbing the peace."

"Law or no law, I want you out."

"Not until I get my property back."

"She isn't yours," Mr. Fraunces said. "You can't prove that."

"Oh yes I can," the other man said. "She's mine, and I'm going to have her."

Well, that froze my spine, because there wasn't nobody he could be talking about but me. I dropped the potato I was peeling, and the knife, and jumped up. The first cook swiveled around. "You just set right where you are, Nosey," she snapped.

"He's after me," I said. "I got to hide." I skipped around the heap of potatoes, heading for the kitchen door. I didn't know where I was going, I was just going. I shot for the door, and just as I was about there the third cook leaped after me and caught ahold of me by the back of my skirt. I was plenty scared. "Let me go," I shouted. "He's going to take me away and sell me off south."

"You calm down, Nosey," the third cook said.

Then the kitchen door slammed open, and in they come, some man I'd never seen before, with Mr. Fraunces right after him. "If you don't get out of my place in two minutes I'll have you thrown out."

The man didn't pay no attention to Mr. Fraunces. "There she is," he said, pointing his finger at me. He was thin and maybe fifty years old, and when he spoke his face didn't move no matter what he said, but stayed still as ice on a pond. "She's mine. I want her," he said.

Mr. Fraunces raised his hands to grab for the man. "Out of here, Ivers. Out of my place."

I broke loose from the third cook and swung around behind her so the man couldn't get at me. Mr. Fraunces raised his hand to grab for him. "Out of here, Ivers," he shouted. "Out of here before I throw you out."

It was Captain Ivers. I began to tremble and shake. I

44

made another leap for the kitchen door, but the third cook grabbed ahold of me again. I began to squirm and twist to get loose.

But Mr. Fraunces made a snatch at Captain Ivers. Ivers backed away toward the dining room where he'd come from. "I'll have the law on you, Fraunces," he said, the words coming sharp as pebbles out of that frozen face.

"You'd better be able to prove it, Ivers," Mr. Fraunces said.

"I will," Captain Ivers said. "The next time I will." And he turned and walked out of the kitchen.

I was so weak and surprised, I had to lean against the kitchen door to stay on my feet.

I couldn't understand none of it. "Mr. Fraunces," I said, "was that really Captain Ivers?"

"Yes," he said.

"Why was he after me?"

Mr. Fraunces looked around at the cooks. Then he said, "Carrie, come down to my office." He turned and went out of the kitchen through the dining room. I followed along, feeling confused and nervous. He went out of the dining room and down the hall, and then into the office. He sat down at his shiny desk, and I stood beside it on his fancy carpet. I could see the kitchen yard through his window, with the sun shining down on the chickens that was scratching around there. I wondered what it would be like to be a chicken and have no worries except where to lay the next egg.

Mr. Fraunces leaned back in his chair with his hands

45

behind his head and looked at me for a couple of minutes. I listened to the clock tick and thought about the chickens. Then he leaned forward and put his arms on the desk. "Ivers thinks he has a claim to you," he said.

"Why, sir? I don't understand nothing about it. I never saw him before."

He shook his head. "It's what I've been worried about for years. He was bound to come after you sooner or later."

"But why?" I said. "Why me?"

"I'm not exactly sure what the legal grounds are," he said. "There's parts of it I don't understand. Too many of the people involved are dead. I don't think Jack Arabus knew the whole story. And he was drowned a long time ago, anyway."

Suddenly something fantastic struck me. "Sir, I ain't Dan's sister, am I?"

He shook his head. "No, that's not it. I don't believe that's it, anyway. Jack always said that your father had been killed in the fighting."

"But why is Captain Ivers after me?"

"I'm not sure what his reason is. He figures he's got the law on his side, some way. But we won't know exactly what his scheme is until he shows his hand."

"Do you think he can get me, sir?"

Mr. Fraunces looked mighty grim. "That's what's worried me all along. I think the law might say so." He shook his head. "I just don't know."

46

# 6

ABOUT TWO DAYS LATER the *Junius Brutus* docked at Peck's Slip, and in the evening Dan come around to visit. There wasn't nothing to do on the ship when it was in port and besides, at the tavern he was allowed to eat whatever he wanted, because of Mr. Fraunces thinking so high of him. So he come, and I sat out back with him in the kitchen yard while he stuffed himself with oyster stew and cold steak left over from supper.

"Well, I can't understand it at all, Carrie," he said. "I never in my life heard Captain Ivers mention your name. He kept it all to himself."

"But why did he light on me, Dan?"

"That's the question, isn't it? He must have figured out he has some claim to you, and he's bound to get you

47

and sell you. He could get three hundred dollars for you, I reckon."

It was queer being worth that much money, and not have any of it for yourself. "It has something to do with your daddy, Dan," I said.

"Did you ask Mr. Fraunces?" Dan said.

"He said he don't know much about it, but I figure he knows more than he's saying."

"Do you think he'd tell me?" Dan said.

"He ain't here," I said. "He went over to New Jersey after some vegetables." I wasn't going to tell Dan that standing in Mr. Fraunces' office I'd got the idea that I might be Dan's sister. "It has something to do with your daddy and my daddy being friends, and then my daddy being killed."

"Carrie, that's just a story you made up. You don't know that. Willy's daddy was killed in the war, too, and that didn't make them friends. Of course they *was* friends, because my Ma and Willy's Ma were sisters. But it wasn't on account of they were both soldiers."

But I wanted to puzzle it out bad, and I couldn't give up. "Tell me about your daddy again."

He shrugged. "I already told you a dozen times, Carrie. He belonged to Captain Ivers, and Ivers sent him off to fight instead of going himself. So after six years of fighting, the law said daddy was free, but Captain Ivers claimed it wasn't so, and got the sheriff to put him in jail. That was when my daddy went to court and proved he had a right to be free."

"And Willy helped him."

"Willy risked herself to bring him his papers that saved him."

"And he got famous because he took a rich white man to court and won the case."

"My daddy, he wasn't afraid of any white man. He fought right next to General Washington at the Battle of Trenton. General Washington himself signed my daddy's papers."

He was about to tell that old story about his daddy leading General Washington's horse across a stream and saving his life, or whatever it was, so I jumped in. "And that's why Captain Ivers was bound and determined to catch Willy and sell her off South. He hated her for helping your daddy get free?"

"There was more to it. She had a terrible fight with Ivers. She blamed him for letting her Ma die, because he wouldn't get her any medicine and she jumped on him and scratched his face. Oh, he'd give anything to get her."

"But what right has he got to Willy? She ain't his slave."

"He doesn't have any right. He just wants to get her," Dan said.

"And what right does he have to me?" It was making me pretty mad. I had never even seen the man until two days before, and he was trying to ruin my whole life. It's what you got for being black—the whites could do anything they wanted to and you couldn't say nothing about it. "It ain't fair," I said.

"He figures he's got the law on his side some way, I

49

reckon," Dan said. "White folks own the law. You know that, Carrie."

"Your daddy got himself free with the law."

"That's so," he said. "But it don't happen that way very often."

He finished off the stew, and began licking the bowl. "That's mighty good stew," he said. "I believe I'll have some more."

"The first cook ain't going to like that."

"I don't pay any attention to the cooks," he said. He got up.

"I still can't figure out how your daddy fits into it," I said. "If he ain't my Pa, how did he get ahold of me?"

"I don't reckon we'll ever know, Carrie." And he walked off toward the kitchen.

It didn't matter to Dan if I didn't know who my Ma and Pa was, but I had to know. I just *had* to know. I was determined I'd find out some day. Who could they be? I was just starting to wonder about that again, when here come Dan back out of the kitchen on the run, with his stew bowl still empty. He raced up to me. "Carrie," he said in a sort of loud whisper, "he's here. You got to hide, quick."

"Who? Who?"

"Ivers. He's got some kind of paper and a sheriff and he's going to take you away."

I jumped up, scared as could be.

"Quick," Dan said.

I ran across the kitchen yard and into the barn which was full of shadows. Just as I got inside, I heard the kitchen door bang open and that cold voice of Captain Ivers shout, "Arabus. Dan Arabus. What are you doing here?"

"Just visiting, sir," I heard Dan say. I slipped through the shadows in the barn, past the cows that was tethered, and the chickens asleep on their roosts, to the ladder that went up to the haymow.

"Where's that nigger girl?" Captain Ivers said.

"I don't know, sir," Dan said. "I ain't seen her."

I heard a cracking sound, and I knew he'd slapped Dan across the face. I jumped to the ladder and climbed up as quick as I dared for the noise. "You're a liar, Arabus," Captain Ivers said. "You've always been a liar. Where is she?"

"No, sir," he said. "I ain't seen her at all. I just got here a few minutes ago." I could hear the cooks a twittering and jabbering away all in a state because of Captain Ivers come to take me away.

Then I was up in the hayloft. I crawled across the heaped-up hay to the back of the loft, where it was near pitch dark, and slid down into the hay. I couldn't hear anything anymore, except my breathing and my heart thumping away like mad. Then by and by I heard some clumping around down on the floor of the barn, and saw a light faintly flashing on the roof above, and I knew they was searching the barn. Their voices was muffled, but I could make out words like "Over there," and "Swing the light here," and then finally: "Try the hayloft."

I lay dead still, letting my breath slip in and out over

51

my lips as easy as I could. Now I wished I'd thought more serious about running away. There was footsteps on the ladder coming up, and then suddenly through the loose hay over my face a light flashed in my eyes. I closed them, and lay there praying. Then I heard a voice say, "She ain't up here," and the footsteps clumped down the ladder. I took in a suck of breath so big I figured they was bound to hear it, but they didn't. And by and by the clumping around died off and it was quiet. I waited, and waited, and then I crawled out of there as easy as I could, and slipped over to the ladder. Still no noise. I climbed down the ladder and tiptoed over to the barn door and looked out into the kitchen yard. Nobody was there, but now I could hear voices coming from the kitchen. It sounded to me like Mr. Fraunces was back.

I raced across the kitchen yard and peeked in a window. It was Mr. Fraunces all right, standing in the kitchen with three cooks around him jabbering away and waving their arms, and Mr. Fraunces looking mighty grim. So I went to the door and walked in. When Mr. Fraunces saw me, he swooped over, picked me up and give me a hug. It felt mighty good: Mr. Fraunces wasn't much of a one for hugging people.

"They didn't find me," I said. "I hid in the hayloft."

"Thank the Lord," he said. "But we've got to get you someplace safe." He put me down and stood there looking at me and thinking. And by and by he said, "Carrie, do you suppose you could behave yourself if I took you with me to the President's house?"

Well, that hit me like I was struck over the head with a brick. I couldn't believe I heard it right. "What, sir?"

"I said, do you suppose you could behave yourself if I took you with me to President Washington's house?"

Well, I had to believe it. "Oh yes sir, *yes* sir." I heard the first cook take in a breath like she'd been hit. "Yes sir, I'd be as good as pie and wouldn't fool around nor break nothing—"

"And work hard and wash more frequently than at present?"

"—and go to church and say my prayers regular—"

"And tell the truth and mind when you're bid to do something?"

"—and not sass anybody nor have impure—"

He laughed and held up his hand. "Just so long as you keep them to yourself is enough." He considered. "I think I'll do it," he said finally. "You'll be a lot safer there."

# 7

WELL, THE COOKS, they could hardly stand it. They puffed out their cheeks and stumped around the kitchen, and when they put down a pot they didn't just set it down, but banged it on the table, all the while muttering under their breath about how it beat all and what was the world coming to, and who'd have believed it in a thousand years, and cursing a good deal, too, until between the pots banging and the cursing it sounded like an artillery drill around there. I didn't say nothing, but stayed quiet and did everything I was told, which was something new every two minutes. But inside I was smiling.

After we finished serving supper, me and Horace took our plates outside the way we usually done when the weather was favorable so's to be away from the cooks. I told him about it. It shook him some, too. He frowned. Then he said, "Well, I expect I'll go to President Washington's, too. It's just that Mr. Fraunces hasn't got around to telling me yet."

"Well I hope you do, Horace," I said. I did hope he would go, when the time come, because it would give me a friend over there. But for now I didn't mind having something Horace didn't have for a change.

"Yes, that's it," he said. "Mr. Fraunces don't want to let it out too soon, for fear the other waiters will be jealous."

"That's probably it," I said.

"I'm sure of it," he said. "I don't mean nothing by it, Carrie, but it don't seem likely he'd take a plain kitchen maid and leave behind somebody who is generally held to be the best waiter in New York, and is a prince at writing, besides."

I was tired of him always saying I wasn't nothing but a kitchen maid. "You can't cipher," I said. "Dan can cipher."

"Oh, I could cipher if I wanted to. There ain't nothing to it, once you know. All you got to do is set your mind to it. I ain't had the time for it. Once I get around to it, it won't be nothing for me to learn."

"Dan can count as high as he wants, too." I said. "Hundreds and hundreds."

"Why there ain't nothing to that, Carrie. I can count as high as I want, too."

"Let's hear you count to a hundred," I said.

"Oh, I can do that, easy. And I would, too, but it'd take too long."

"Dan—"

He frowned. "Never mind about Dan." Then suddenly he reached into his jacket pocket. "With all this chattering you made me forget I got a letter from Willy." He took it out, unfolded it, and handed it over to me. Of course, it didn't mean anything to me. It was just squiggles on a page. "Read it to me, Horace."

He rustled the paper around and frowned over it and he read it out real slow. "Dear Horace, I meaned to write sooner, but it takes me so long. I am reading pretty good. Ever day I read a story out of the newspaper. I write down the hard words and ask someone about them when I get a chance. I got a new job. Cook at a tavin. I wist I was back home. I miss everybody. I don't dare come yet. Write if Captain Ivers goes back to Stratford to stay for good. Willy."

He read it so slow that sometimes he come to a complete stop and had to back up a little to get going again. It took near five minutes for him to get through it. But he done it and then he was quiet and I knew he was trying to think up some way he could get her back to New York. He missed her a lot more than he wanted to tell anybody. He was in love with her. I wondered if she was in love with him. When you come down to it, Horace was all right. If you scraped off all that shining and puffing, Horace was all right. He wouldn't steal anything from you, or cheat you, or take unfair advan-

56

tage. Of course, he was tight with his money. He saved every penny he got and wouldn't lend nobody nothing, nor buy nobody cakes or punch. Once he bought Willy some ribbons for her hair and it shocked the cooks so much they couldn't talk about anything else for days. They knew from that he was in love, and they teased him about it so much he never done anything like it again; or if he did, he never told nobody. But leaving aside the puffing, and being tight, Horace was all right, and I thought Willy might be in love with him, too. If it had been me, I'd have picked Dan over Horace any time.

In the end, Horace didn't get to go to President Washington's house. Mr. Fraunces took only me and the second cook. He said that the first cook and the rest had to stay to keep the tavern going, which was going to be under the hand of his wife. He said that the second cook would do all right; he would cook the cakes and puddings for President Washington himself. And so I left the tavern.

President Washington had moved into a house on Cherry Street, over near the East River, which had belonged to a rich man named Samuel Osgood. It was mighty grand, a big brick house three stories high, with four great windows across the front. There was a slew of servants there—white servants and black ones, too, that President Washington had brought up from his home in Virginia. And all sorts of coaches and a dozen horses and the whole house just filled with stacks of fancy furniture and china and endless silver and carpets and such. Oh, it was the grandest place I'd ever seen.

My work was mostly washing dishes and cleaning the kitchen and gleaming things in the dining room. I didn't hardly go anywhere else in the house. I was kept mighty busy, too, for there was always something going on around there. Besides the President and Mrs. Washington there was their two grandchildren. Some men who worked in government lived there, too, so as to be handy when the President wanted them. There was always people in and out. I was supposed to stay out of sight, mostly, but sometimes when I was out in the dining room gleaming something, I'd see people go by in the hall. I recognized some of them from seeing them at the tavern. Mr. Alexander Hamilton, he come around to see the President a lot. So did Mr. Thomas Jefferson. It was funny to see them together, for Mr. Jefferson, he was very tall and Mr. Hamilton was very short and hardly come up to Mr. Jefferson's chin. But no matter, he was just as important as Mr. Jefferson.

I wondered about that. How come tall folks wasn't more important than short folks? White folks was more important than black folks, but white folks hadn't done nothing to make themselves white any more than tall folks had to make themselves tall. It didn't seem to me that someone should be more important just because of how they was born. You ought to *do* something to get important.

There was guests for dinner most every night. On Tuesdays the President had a levee at which a lot of ambassadors and congressmen and such come and sat around the dining room and talked about the government. On Fridays Mrs. Washington had her drawing rooms, where all the rich people in New York, dressed up fancy as could be, gabbled and gossiped and drank tea and coffee and ate cakes and candy. It was a powerful lot of work getting everything ready for the levees and drawing rooms, because everything had to gleam like the sun. And it was even more work cleaning up afterward, what with having to wash forty cups and forty saucers and forty cake plates and forty knives and forty forks and everything else. But I was mighty proud to be working for the President, and happy to be where Captain Ivers didn't know where I was, too.

Of course the President didn't pay me no attention. I saw him a lot, getting into his coach or sitting at his dinner when the waiters swung the door to the dining room open. But he didn't come into the kitchen. If he wanted something done, he sent his secretary, Mr. Lear, around to tell Mr. Fraunces, and Mr. Fraunces would tell us. But once I did talk to the President.

One of the delivery boys had spilled a box of strawberries by the side door and I was out there helping to clean up. As we was doing it, President Washington's carriage came along and stopped so's the President could get out and go in the side door. Me and the delivery boy skipped out of the way. When the President passed by us, the delivery boy bowed and I curtsied as best I could for never having no training at it. Just then the President's handkerchief

59

fell out of his sleeve. He didn't notice it, but walked on. I jumped forward, picked it up, and caught up with him. "Sir," I said.

He stopped and looked at me. I held out the handkerchief. "Sir, you dropped this."

"Oh yes, thank you," he said, in that serious way he had. "Who are you?"

I tried another curtsy, which wasn't no more successful than the first one. "Carrie, sir. I come from Mr. Fraunces' tavern."

"I see," he said. He patted me on the head, took the handkerchief, and gave me a copper. Then he marched on into the house. That was the only time I talked to him. He looked mighty serious. I figured being president of a brand-new country that didn't have no rules yet wasn't no bushel of roses.

Of course, I missed the tavern some. I missed Horace and the other waiters, and I even missed the other cooks, who was all right in their way, even if they was too bossy and always telling you to look sharp.

Horace come around sometimes with a message for Mr. Fraunces or something, and I usually had a chance to gab with him and get caught up on the news: whether the third cook had fallen asleep and burned the eggs again, or what famous people had come in for dinner. Sometimes he had news of Dan, too. Dan come around to the tavern whenever he could same as always. I told Horace, "I wished he'd come around and see me, too."

"Well he probably would, Carrie, but you can't just

go dropping by the President's mansion like it was a cow barn."

"Tell him the President won't mind. There's so much food left over after dinner the President wouldn't notice if he ate for days."

"Yes, but Mr. Fraunces would."

"Well, tell him anyway," I said.

I missed Dan a lot. But aside from that, after I got to know the people around the Cherry Street house, I got comfortable. President Washington had brought up from his plantation in Virginia seven slaves—three for the stables, and four to help in the house. The boss of them was old Will Lee, who was crippled in the legs and drank a good deal, but had been George Washington's body servant for just years and years and was mighty close to him. Old Will, he didn't pay no attention to me; I was nothing to him. But some of the others was more friendly and I'd sit around and chat with them when we ate our supper.

They talked a lot about George Washington's plantation, which was called Mount Vernon and was down in Virginia someplace, hundreds of miles away. Leastwise I supposed it was hundreds of miles away—I didn't know for sure. Oh, they said it was the grandest place, with hundreds of slaves and wheat and cornfields as far as you could see, and no end of horses and stables and servants. The Cherry Street house wasn't nothing compared to it, they said.

They was mighty scornful about New York, too. "What's wrong with New York?" I said.

"Oh, New York ain't a fit place to live. It's dirty and noisy and smells so bad you hardly dare breathe."

"It ain't that bad," I said. "You got to get used to it."

"Used to it? Why, who could get used to open sewers running down the middle of the streets and dead animals left where they lay and people just walking around them and paying no attention."

"They don't leave the animals lay," I said. "The carters pick them up. Anyway, you ain't got no great buildings like we have, and all these fine houses, and such."

"Well, it don't matter," one of the older ones said. "We ain't staying here anyways."

Well, that surprised me a good deal. "We ain't staying here?"

"No, we ain't. I got it from old Will that the Congress is aiming to move the government out of New York."

"No," I said. "Not after they spent all that money fixing up City Hall for it."

"It don't matter. Old Will says we're going."

"Where to?"

He shrugged. "They don't rightly know. Philadelphia, maybe. Virginia maybe. They ain't decided yet. But old Will says we're going, and he got it from President Washington himself."

I didn't know what to think about that. 'Course maybe Mr. Fraunces wouldn't go, and if he did maybe he wouldn't take me. But it seemed like old Will said we

62

was all going. I wasn't safe in New York; but I didn't think I'd be any better off in Virginia. Down in Virginia if I done something wrong, which wasn't no more likely to happen than the sun would come up on Wednesday, they might stick me out in the cornfields to hoe the rest of my life away. Besides, New York was my home. I was used to it, and I liked it, even if there was dead animals flung around it and Captain Ivers was scouting around for me.

On the other side of it, if I was to go someplace else I would be safe from Captain Ivers. And maybe we'd go to Philadelphia instead of Virginia. Now Horace, he'd jump at the chance to go to Philadelphia. Sometimes he'd come over to Cherry Street with a message for Mr. Fraunces from his wife, who was managing the tavern. If I was out in the dining room gleaming things, he'd slip out there and stare around at the cabinet shelves lined up with silver dishes and the china with the pictures on it, and the sconces on the walls, and the grandfather clock in the corner that I had to polish once a week. It made his mouth water just to look. He'd say, "Carrie, I'm blamed if I can understand how they chose you for this job. I don't mean nothing by that, you do the best you can, but when it comes to setting up a dining room, why that's meat and drink to me. I been doing it for years at the most famous tavern in New York, and I can't be beat at it. You'll admit that yourself, Carrie."

Well, he hadn't been at it for years—only three years. He'd been a stableboy for ten years before that, and knew more about setting up a stable than a dining room so far as that went. But all I'd say was, "Oh, I'll admit it, Horace, there ain't much you can be beat at."

And he'd give me a look and say, "Don't you get sassy with me, Carrie. I don't care if you do work for the President, you ain't supposed to be sassing me."

But like I said, the worst part of being at the President's mansion was not seeing Dan. He didn't come, and he didn't come. But then one cold November day, when there was frost on the windows, and I could see my breath in the kitchen yard, he came. I was in the kitchen peeling potatoes—it didn't much seem to matter where I worked, there was always potatoes. In come one of the stableboys, and walked over to me. "There's somebody out in the barn who wants to see you, Carrie," he said in a low voice so the cooks wouldn't hear.

"Who is it?" I said.

"A nigger sailor," the stable boy said. "He said you'd know."

My heart jumped, and I began to glow inside. It had to be Dan. I gave the cook a look. She was busy by the fire and wasn't paying me no attention, so I just skidded out of there without asking no questions.

It was Dan all right, standing in the stable door sort of lounging up against the jamb. I dashed over to him and he hugged me, and I hugged him back, and didn't want to let go of him, neither, until he near squeezed the breath out of me.

"How did you get away, Dan?"

"I slipped off the ship," he said. "I've only got a minute. I got something to tell you."

"You can always come here," I said. "It don't matter to President Washington."

"Carrie, listen to me. I only got a little time. I found out something about you."

"About me?"

"You remember when Captain Ivers came to the tavern and you hid in the hayloft? Well, he had a sheriff with him, and a piece of paper that was supposed to prove that you belonged to him. He clouted me, and then he started shouting to the sheriff to look for you in the barn and such, and didn't pay attention to me. And the way he was holding the paper folded up I was able to read what was on the outside of it."

"You could?" That excited me some.

"Well, just the name up in the corner. It was William Samuel Johnson."

"Dr. Johnson? Your Dr. Johnson? The one who's holding your notes for you?"

"It has to be," he said. "It can't be anybody else."

"That's all you saw?" I was kind of disappointed.

"Well, it's something," he said.

I stood there trying to puzzle it out. "It don't make any sense to me at all," I said.

"It's something," he said again.

"What do you make of it?"

"I don't know exactly," he said. "But my daddy, he worked for Dr. Johnson once. He knew Dr. Johnson.

He's a big lawyer, and what I figure is, my daddy got him to draw up some kind of paper for him about you."

"What kind of paper?"

"Well, I don't know. But it seems like it's got to be that a-way. I mean my daddy brought you to Mr. Fraunces' tavern. He must have known who you was, and he got Dr. Johnson to draw it up on a piece of paper."

Suddenly I wasn't so disappointed anymore. "Why, Dan, you can ask him about it next time you see him."

"I'm going to, Carrie. Soon as I get a chance. I got to go. I only slipped off the ship for just a minute."

He turned and started to go. I grabbed his arm. "Dan, you can come here any time you want. The President, he don't mind."

He nodded. "I'll come when I can. Soon as I find out something more from Dr. Johnson." Then he left.

# 8

WELL, IT WAS the most bothersome thing that had ever happened to me. Knowing just a little bit about who I was and where I'd come from was worse than knowing nothing at all. If you'd never seen any strawberry tarts you wouldn't think much about them one way or another, and it wouldn't bother you that you didn't have any. But if they was in the shops and every time you went by you could see them, and smell them all hot and sweet through an open window, why you'd get so you couldn't hardly think of anything else. First I found out that Jack Arabus was mixed up with me some way. Now it seemed like Dr. William Samuel Johnson was in on it, too. But how? Why? It kept coming back to me that maybe Jack Arabus was my father, and I was Dan's sister, even though Mr. Fraunces said I wasn't.

Maybe Jack Arabus had another wife somewheres that he didn't tell nobody about, because you wasn't supposed to have but one wife. But I wasn't sure. I wasn't sure of nothing.

Meanwhile, there was rumors about everything: rumors that the notes was going up and rumors that the notes was going down; rumors that we was going south and rumors that we was staying in New York; and the rumors was divided into a half dozen smaller rumors about where we was going. One night, we was eating supper with the Mount Vernon servants talking about what it was like in Philadelphia when one of them said, "It ain't going to matter to you, Nosey, you ain't going no place, anyway."

"I'll go if Mr. Fraunces tells me to go. I belong to him."

He gave me a long look. "Mr. Fraunces ain't going no place, either."

"What do you mean?" I said. "He'll go wherever the President goes."

"No he won't. The President's getting ready to get another steward. He's going to dismiss Fraunces."

I started to get angry that anybody would say such a thing about Mr. Fraunces. "It ain't true."

"That's what old Will says."

"Why would the President want to send Mr. Fraunces away? Everybody says he sets the best table in the United States."

"That's the problem, old Will says. He says the President believes Fraunces is spending too much money.

Will says the President don't like extravagance. Will says he watches the money close. He says the President don't see the need for three or four different wines at dinner, nor five or six dishes when two would do. The President, he don't eat but two dishes at a meal himself, and he don't see why anybody needs five or six. Look at dinner today. First soup, then a roasted fish and a boiled one, then a smoked ham, and fowl and no end of dessert—apple pie, pudding that Fraunces made himself, jelly, ice cream, pecan pie, white cake, brandied peaches, nuts. Why, there was enough food to kill a regiment. The President don't like it. It's a waste, he says."

I could see the point. It *was* a waste. A powerful lot of food come back into the kitchen after dinner every day. Oh, the servants ate it, so's it didn't spoil and get thrown away. But it was a waste to give all that fancy food to servants, who didn't expect but pork and porridge or fish chowder or some such, and would have been content with that. Why, they even got left-over wine, sometimes two or three kinds. Of course, the whole idea of dismissing Mr. Fraunces might just be rumors, too. But it worried me some. If Mr. Fraunces went back to the tavern, like as not he'd take me back, too. And then sure as anything, Captain Ivers would find out, and come after me again. Oh, it was worrisome.

'Midst all the rumors a week went by, and Dan didn't come with any more news about who I was. I was mighty impatient, but there wasn't nothing I could do about it. There was no way of telling when he would get a chance to skid off from the *Junius Brutus*.

Then one evening he came. It was pretty late on a snowy December night. The President and his family usually went to bed at nine and sometimes earlier, because they got up by five o'clock or before. The cooks was gone, too, and Mr. Fraunces had just left to go back to the tavern. I was about ready to go to bed myself, when the kitchen door opened and Dan come in, the wind and snow swirling in the open door behind him. He was snow all over, and cold, and he come right to the fire and stood there warming himself.

"Did you find out anything from Dr. Johnson about me, Dan?"

"I'm sorry, Carrie," he said. "I know how fired up you are to find out who you are, but I don't know anything more. I just come from seeing him about my notes, and I asked him about you. He said it was true that he'd drawn up some papers for my daddy, he remembered doing it, but he couldn't remember anything about them. It was years ago, he said. He couldn't remember that far back."

"Oh," I said. It was mighty disappointing.

"Don't be too sad, Carrie," Dan said. "Dr. Johnson, he said when he had a chance he'd look through his papers and see if there was anything about you in them."

"When, Dan? When?"

Dan shook his head. "He's mighty busy, Carrie. You know he's president of the college and also a senator in

70

the new Congress. I don't know when he'll have the chance."

Well, it was a disappointment. But I didn't want to show it, for fear Dan would think I was blaming him for it. So I got him a nice piece of veal pie and some bread and beer and we pulled our stools up close to the fire, which was dying down, and sat there in the shadows with the cold wind outside giving a good whistle from time to time, like it was calling somebody and didn't know who. I watched Dan eat the veal pie and drink the beer, and between times toast bread on a long fork and smear it with blackberry jam. And to take my mind off my troubles, I asked Dan what Dr. Johnson had said about his notes.

"He said he didn't know any more than anybody else what would happen to them. It would depend on the new government and there was no telling what they would do. I wish they'd make up their minds one way or another. I don't think I can stand this much longer."

"Since there ain't nothing you can do about it, Dan, I think you ought to put it straight out of your mind."

"I know I should, Carrie. I know I should do that. But blamed if I can. It just keeps coming back."

"Maybe you'd best sell them while they're worth something."

"I don't know, Carrie."

"What would you do if they wasn't worth nothing at all in the end?"

He looked mighty grim and shook his head. "I'd run

71

off," he said. "I wouldn't have no choice. I'd run off, and hope that somehow I could get Ma free, too."

Well, that scared me some. If Dan run off he might go up to some place like Massachusetts or even Canada, where he'd be free. Of course, in Massachusetts if your owner found out where you was and went to court to get you back, the law would send you back, but you wouldn't be easy to find. I didn't want to think about that, so I changed the subject. "There's a rumor from the Mount Vernon folks that the President's going to let Mr. Fraunces go."

"I don't see how that could be," Dan said. "Mr. Fraunces runs the most famous tavern in New York. He's got to be best for a steward."

"That's the trouble," I said. "He wants everything just so, and plenty of it—four or five different wines at a meal and a half dozen dishes. The President, he says it's a waste. He likes things plain, and don't eat but two dishes at a meal."

"Well, there's a point—" Dan started to say, but just then the kitchen door banged open and in come Horace, the wind and snow swirling in behind him. We was mighty surprised to see him.

Horace said that when Mr. Fraunces was on his way back to the tavern he seen Dan coming along to the President's mansion, and he told Horace.

"Dan," Horace said, "Mr. Fraunces says Captain Ivers is planning to take the *Junius Brutus* down to Philadelphia."

"Why yes, that's so," Dan said.

"I figure you could carry a letter down to Willy. I figured I'd better warn her that Captain Ivers is down there."

"I might not have a chance to find her, Horace."

"But you might."

"I might. I'll take the letter and if I don't find her, maybe I'll run across somebody who knows her and can deliver the letter to her."

So I got Horace some of the veal pie and Dan gave him the toasting fork, and while Horace was getting warm and comfortable I fetched a bottle of ink and a sheet of paper out of the pantry where Mr. Fraunces kept them for making out his menus and things. And while he was getting his bread toasted, I said, "Horace, there's a whole lot of rumors going around that the President is getting ready to let Mr. Fraunces go."

"It's true," Horace said. "Mr. Fraunces said so himself. He said that the President didn't hold with such fanciness as Mr. Fraunces wanted. He says the President of the United States ought to set the best table in the country, never mind what it cost. He says President Washington can dismiss him or kill him, but he's bound and determined to set the best table in America as long as he's steward."

Then, when Horace had stoked up on toast and veal pie, he set himself down at the table, and begun to write his letter, scratching and splattering the ink and blaming the pen and the paper and I don't know what all for the mess he was making. As he wrote, he said the words out loud. "Dear—Willy—I—am—mighty—" He stopped and chewed on the end of the pen for a minute. Then he said, "Say, Dan, I'll bet you don't know how to spell *mighty*."

"Sure I do," Dan said, shoving another piece of toast on the fork.

"Let's hear you do it, then."

"Of course he knows how to spell it," I said. "Don't you believe him?"

"I believe him," Horace said. "I just want to hear him do it. There's more than one way to do it."

"There isn't but one way that I know of," Dan said.

"That's all you know, Dan," Horace said. "I seen it spelled a half dozen different ways."

"Sure, but only one of them was right."

"Well, that's the question, isn't it," Horace said. "Which one do you think is right?"

"Why, it's m-i-g-h-t-y."

Horace swooped down with the pen and wrote it out. Then he tipped the page down to the fire and had a good look at it. "M-i-g-h-t-y," he said. "That ain't right, Dan. That *g* don't belong in there, that's clear enough. I ain't sure about the *h*, neither."

"Yes they do," Dan said. "That's the way it's spelled."

"Well, it looks mighty peculiar to me," Horace said. "I could tolerate the *h*, maybe, because an *h* don't pronounce much anyway and you can take it or leave it."

"It pronounces pretty well at the front of your own name, Horace," Dan said.

74

"Oh sure," he said. "That's because it's at the front. When *h* is at the front, you got to pronounce it. Everybody knows that. But hidden down in the middle of a word it don't hardly matter at all. It just rushes by like a tassel of air, so's you don't hardly notice it. But *g* is different. A *g* is a real pronouncer. You can't skip by it the way you can skip by an *h*. It stands out. It's like a hook there in a word and it catches you up as it goes by." He shook his head. "No, Dan, that *g* don't belong there." And he scratched it out.

Dan finished toasting his piece of bread and smeared it up with blackberry jam. "Do as you like, Horace. It's a free country. I reckon you can spell it any way you want."

But Horace had got back to the letter. "Mighty— worried—if—you—was—all—right."

Dan took a bite of toast and said in a muffled voice, "Horace, how're you spelling *right*?"

Horace gave Dan a look. "Why, r-i-t-e. Any fool knows that."

"You wouldn't put a *g* in there, would you?"

"What fool would put a *g* in there?" Horace said.

"Most fools I know," Dan said. "It belongs in there."

Horace stared down at the letter. Then he shook his head. "No," he said. "There's no place to fit a *g* in there, Dan. It won't go." And he went on writing. "Captain— Ivers—is—coming—to—Philadelphia." He looked at Dan. "Now there's one I bet you can't spell, Dan."

"I bet I can, too," Dan said. "I been to Philadelphia."

"That don't mean you can spell it."

75

"Let's hear you spell it, Horace," Dan said.

"That'd just give it away to you, Dan. Let's hear you do it."

Dan, he sort of grinned and said, "P-h-i-l-a—"

Horace slammed his pen down on the board and leaned back and looked at Dan. "Dan, you beat just about everything. I never seen anybody for jamming in letters where they don't belong. You don't need no *p* or no *h* in *Philadelphia*. The way you throw letters around you'd think there was no end of them. It's just a waste." He shook his head. "I ain't never seen nothing like it."

"Well, Horace," Dan said, "I always admired a man who went his own way, regardless. But you got an advantage on me. You're free and can spell any way you want. I ain't free and have got to do it the way I'm told. It makes all the difference."

76

# 9

I⊤ ⊤ook Horace near an hour to write the letter, even though there wasn't much to it. The idea of it was that Horace wanted to quit working at Fraunces Tavern and go down to Philadelphia. He didn't say so, but I knew he figured that once he was down there he'd get Willy to marry him. He'd be sorry to leave Fraunces', I knew that because Mr. Fraunces had always treated him right; but he was so all-fired in love with Willy that nothing would stop him.

He wanted to know from Willy how things was for black folks down there. Was there any good jobs for free blacks, was there any chance of setting up a tavern, or getting into some other kind of business? Horace had saved up considerable money, which Mr. Fraunces was keeping for him in his safe. Horace never

77

let on how much it was, but I knew it was considerable.

I'd miss Horace. It seemed like everybody was going away from me. I didn't know what I'd do if he was gone. I wouldn't have nobody to talk to. Of course, if Mr. Fraunces was let go by President Washington, and I went back to the tavern, I'd have the cooks. But they was white, and it wasn't the same. Besides, I didn't want to go back to the tavern, for fear of Captain Ivers. It would be mighty risky for me. What would I do if I had to go back there? Maybe I would have to run away. I would hate doing that. But maybe I would have to.

I couldn't blame Horace for that, though. He was in love and was bound to marry Willy, no matter what. He wasn't in no hurry, though. Horace, he wasn't one to rush into things. He liked to take his time and look at all sides of it first.

By the time he got the letter finished, I'd dozed off in front of the fire. I woke up when he folded it up and give it to Dan. Dan slipped it under his shirt—if Captain Ivers found it he'd know Willy was in Philadelphia—and went off to the *Junius Brutus*. Then Horace left, and I was alone.

I knew I ought to go to bed, for it was late and I had to be up pretty soon. But I didn't feel like it. I felt sort of low and sad. Horace was getting his life straightened out, and Dan was getting his straightened out, too; at least he would if his notes come out to be worth something. But I was getting nowhere with nothing. I was bound to be a slave all my life, and on top of it, I couldn't even find out who I was. What was it all about? Jack Arabus was part of it and Dr. Johnson was part of it, and even Mr. Fraunces was part of it some way—he'd got me from Jack Arabus. But how? And would Dr. Johnson ever look through his papers to see if he had something about me? He was high and mighty and I wasn't nothing at all. Why would he even think about me? I figured he'd forgot the whole thing already.

I sat there, watching the fire go down, and feeling the chill creep into the room. Finally I shivered, and knew I had to go to bed, or get froze sitting there. I stood up; and just doing something gave me a little courage and I resolved I wouldn't just sit and wait, I'd get Mr. Fraunces to see Dr. Johnson himself. Dr. Johnson wasn't likely to do nothing for me, but he would for Mr. Fraunces. Mr. Fraunces was pretty high and mighty himself.

It took me three days to catch him alone: he was mighty busy and always going off to market to see what was choice. But finally I caught him. I was out in the pantry weighing out some flour for pies, when Mr. Fraunces come out there to check up on supplies. He said, "I've been meaning to see how you were doing, Carrie. No signs of Ivers, I suppose? Dan's been careful not to let him know where you are, I hope."

"Oh, yes, sir, he wouldn't say nothing about it. But he did tell me something that's got me mighty puzzled. He said that the time Captain Ivers come after me with the sheriff when you wasn't there, he was carrying a paper which said I was his slave. Leastwise, that's what it was supposed to be. It was folded up, but Dan got a look at the outside. It had Dr. William Samuel Johnson's name on it."

Mr. Fraunces looked surprised. "It did? Dan was sure about that?"

"Yes, sir," I said. "And when he went down to see Dr. Johnson about his notes, he asked him about it. Dr. Johnson, he told Dan he didn't remember nothing about it. He said he would look in his papers to see if there was anything about me. But sir, I'm afeard he won't. He's too high, and isn't likely to trouble himself about a kitchen slave."

"And you hoped I might talk to him about it?" Mr. Fraunces said.

"Yes, sir," I said. "If you had the chance, and it wasn't too much trouble."

He nodded. "I certainly will when I have the chance," he said. "It's quite possible that Jack Arabus asked Dr. Johnson to draw up some sort of paper about you—who originally owned you, or something of the sort. I'll try to find out."

But I didn't hear no more about it. December went along with Christmas coming up, and we was rushed to death keeping up with the parties and guests and goings-on in general. And then one morning Mr. Fraunces came in and said that Dr. Johnson himself was coming to dinner along with some others, and the President was going to take them all out to the theater afterward.

80

"Sir," I said, "will you have a chance to ask him?"
Mr. Fraunces looked puzzled, and I knew he'd forgotten, too. "If Dr. Johnson has a paper on me."

"Oh, yes," he said. "I'm sorry, that slipped my mind. But I don't think this is the time for it, Carrie. Dr. Johnson will be busy with the President."

That was mighty disappointing. What better chance would there be? When would I ever be this close to Dr. Johnson? Never, most likely. If anyone knew why Dan's daddy brought me to Mr. Fraunces it would be Dr. Johnson. It seemed like he was the whole lock and key to who I was. If Mr. Fraunces wasn't going to ask him, and Dan couldn't find out nothing, there was nobody going to do it. And that left me down and out and going through life never knowin' who I was and just being nobody at all. But then it flashed through my head that there was somebody else who was going to be close enough to Dr. Johnson to talk to him—and that somebody was me, Carrie No-Name herself. And I decided I *would* try to talk to him, no matter what.

But oh my, there were a lot of problems to it. The first was that I didn't know what Dr. Johnson looked like, and wouldn't know which one he was even if he did come. Mr. Fraunces knew, I figured, but during dinner he always stood out in the dining room telling the waiters to fill up somebody's wineglass, or bring out more squash, or whatever it was: there wouldn't be no way I could get him to point Dr. Johnson out.

The second thing was, even if I knew which one Dr. Johnson was, how was I to get into a conversation with him? I wasn't allowed in the dining room when the white folks was eating, for fear I might breathe on them or something, and it wasn't very likely that Dr. Johnson would come marching out to the kitchen and introduce himself just in case somebody wanted to ask him some questions. There was only one way to do it: catch him somewheres before he came into the house, or catch him somewheres after he was finished dinner and was standing outside waiting for his carriage. And the first wasn't no good, because I didn't know who he was.

The only thing I could do, I figured, was to try to find out which one he was during dinner, and then when they was getting ready to go, dash around outside and pretend I was supposed to dust out the carriages, until Dr. Johnson come out and I could speak to him.

And how was I going to find out which one he was during dinner? That was another puzzler. It didn't seem likely that any of the kitchen help would know, although they might. One thing I could do would be to pass as close to the dining room doors as I could when the waiters was going in and out, in hopes that I would hear somebody say, "My, that's a dinged fine shirt you got on there, Dr. Johnson," or "What do you think of the olive pie situation, Dr. Johnson?" But still, it wasn't going to be easy.

All day long I sweated and puzzled over it, but I couldn't come up with anything better. Dinner was at five as usual. Finally at four o'clock Mr. Fraunces told me to get a jar of oil and a rag and give the dining room a quick polish—the tables and chairs and the wainscoting, and even the big grandfather clock that set in the corner. Some of the servants was out there setting the table, and Mr. Fraunces was standing in the middle of things clapping his hands and shouting out directions. I worked away with the rag and polish, over the table and the chairs and the wainscoting. By about ten minutes of five I was working over the grandfather clock, when suddenly it came to me that a person as scrawny as I was could fit inside of it easy.

It was mighty scary to think of. I would get into all sorts of trouble if I was caught. But who would catch me? Nobody at the President's dinner party was likely to be messing around with no grandfather clock. At a dinner party at the President's you was supposed to swell around in your best clothes and talk big about how you was going to put a tax on babies or get up a law against olive pies, which was a mighty good idea to my mind. You wasn't supposed to be looking inside of no grandfather clock. I mean what would President Washington think if you was to look inside of his grandfather clock? He'd be mighty insulted, that's what, and chances are he'd never ask you to one of his dinners again. So nobody would do it—once I was inside the clock I'd be safe enough.

The problem was getting in. There was a little lock set in the door, but there wasn't no key in the lock and I didn't know if it was locked or not. I hooked my little finger in the key hole, and in a moment I'd eased the casing door open enough to realize that it wasn't locked.

I looked around. The servants had most nearly cleared things away. Mr. Fraunces was standing in the middle of the room with his hands on his hips looking around to see that everything was just so. The servants began to bustle away. I looked up at the face of the clock. It was two minutes to five. I went on oiling the casing—the front, the sides, and the front again.

Mr. Fraunces looked over at me. "Finish up quick now, Carrie," he said.

"Yes, sir," I said. "I'm near done."

He turned and went out into the kitchen. Across the room two servants was carrying the brooms and such out of the room. Then I was all alone. A chill went up my back. I swung open the clock door, climbed inside, swung the door closed again, and there I was in the pitch dark. I was just in time, too, for the minute the door clicked shut I heard voices and I knew the guests was coming in.

And at just about the same moment I realized that I was taking up most all of the room inside that clock and there wasn't no way for the pendulum to swing. It was stopped still where it was when I jumped in, up against the left-hand side of the case, and couldn't swing back and forth the way it was supposed to, because I had it blocked. And if the pendulum couldn't swing, the hands wouldn't go around. I'd stopped the clock dead.

It couldn't tick and it couldn't tock and it would go on saying five o'clock for the rest of the time I was in there.

Me and my dinged ideas. Oh my, how I wished I was somewhere else. Anywhere else. It didn't matter to me in the least where I was, so long as I wasn't inside that clock no more. I'd have given anything to be in jail, or down in the West Indies baking my brains out in a cane field, or even up on the gallows having the minister say the last words over me. At least that way my troubles would be over soon.

I sucked in my stomach and tried to pull myself as tight as I could to the back of the clock, but I couldn't make enough room for the pendulum to go by. Next I tried to bend the pendulum out enough so's it would go by me. But I couldn't do that, neither. It wouldn't bend enough to go past my head, and I was fearful that if I tugged at it too hard I'd pull the whole works loose with a crash. There wasn't nothing to do about it. So I let it go and stood there all cramped up praying that nobody would notice that the clock had stopped; or if they did, they would be too polite to mention it at President Washington's dinner party.

It didn't matter anyway, for I was stuck there now. It was mighty close, and the sweat was beginning to come out on my forehead and trickle down my cheeks. And dark: I couldn't see nothing at all. But since I had gone to so much trouble, I figured I'd better make it worthwhile. So I pushed the door open just the tiniest crack, no more'n the width of a quill pen, and put my eye to

85

it. It gave me just a little slice of a view a couple of inches wide right up close, but fanning out to three or four feet across the room.

Oh, scared as I was, it was a pretty sight, all them setting at the table dressed up so fine, the men in their knee britches and waistcoats, the women in their long dresses and shawls. They was all colors of the rainbow, with embroidery and mother-of-pearl buttons and silver buckles shining everywhere. I never seen nothing like it. And which one was Dr. Johnson?

The way the door was angled I could see about one quarter of President Washington from the side. I could see his nose, his forehead, one eye, part of an ear, and a piece of his stomach where it stuck out against the table. Sometimes he swayed back and disappeared except for his foot and his nose. Waiters was always going to and fro, cutting him off from view. But then the view would open up a little and there he'd be—or at least parts of him, anyway.

The trouble was hearing what they were saying. The people was all talking at a great rate, showing how big they was, and what they was going to do about the olive pie situation, and it was pretty hard to make out any single thing. But sometimes somebody would ask George Washington a question and the people nearby would shut up to hear what he said.

One thing they was talking about was the notes, which they sometimes called bonds, which I guess was the same thing. And it was clear enough that it wasn't just poor soldiers, like Dan's daddy, who got stuck with them. The rich had got stuck, too. A lot of them had sold beef and hay and apples and cloth and shoes and all kinds of things to the army. It was the patriotic thing to do, and there was money in it, too, which is always good for patriotism. And now they was stuck just like the soldiers. It was a good sign, I reckoned, for if the rich was stuck, too, they was more likely to push Congress to pay off the notes than if only the poor was stuck.

But still, nobody seemed sure that Congress would do it. Some said the bonds would go up and some said they would go down, and some said they wouldn't do neither but would stay right where they were. And I was pondering all of this and hoping somebody would say, "What do you think of it, Dr. Johnson?" But instead somebody said, "What time do you suppose it to be? We don't want to miss the theater."

It made me uneasy. I tried to make out who had said it, but I couldn't tell.

The next voice said, "It's just five o'clock."

"That can't possibly be right."

"No, it can't, can it? Why bless me, the clock's stopped."

Well, my blood froze, and I gasped so loud I was scared everybody in the room could hear it. But they didn't; and I stood there praying that they was too polite to go messing around with a clock in the middle of President Washington's dinner party.

"Odd that it should have stopped just when everybody came in," the voice said.

"Might have stopped last week as far as it goes."

"Yes, you're right."

Still feeling sort of trembly I give out a soft little sigh, and begun on a new prayer, that they was too polite to tell the President of the United States that his clock was broke. It wasn't none of their business, anyway. Maybe President Washington liked to have his clock behind, so there'd be more time in the day and he could get more work out of the servants, or some such.

Just as I was thinking that I saw a man lean across the table to George Washington, or at least up to his nose and chin. He had a lot of gray hair and brown eyes, and he was smiling. He said something to the President, and the President swiveled around so he was face on to me. He was staring direct at the clock, and I knew he would be mighty surprised to know that the clock was staring back at him. And I got going on a third prayer, which was that he figured he wouldn't want to mess with no broken clock during one of his dinner parties; he'd wait until the guests had all gone home, which any sensible person would do.

I had got about that far in my prayer, when George Washington smiled, got up, and started to walk toward the clock, with the other man coming along beside him, and a lot of others watching to see what was going on. The sweat was cascading off me now, my heart was racing, and my legs so weak it was all I could do to keep from sitting straight down. I pulled the little door shut and tried to find some way to grip it to hold it tight, so they'd think it was locked. But there was nothing to grip it with. I heard the President say, "Dr. Johnson, that clock has always been my favorite, it doesn't lose as much as a minute a day." I near dropped dead.

Dr. Johnson said, "Perhaps a mouse has built a nest in the works." Then the door swung open and the light came flooding in, and there was me and the President of the United States staring at each other face to face.

# 10

WELL, HIS EYEBROWS shot up and his jaw dropped and
he stood there staring at me. Everybody else got up and
gathered around and stared, too. I blushed as hot as
could be. My head was emptied out clean. I couldn't
think of nothing to do but curtsy, which was a mistake,
because there wasn't no room to curtsy inside a grandfather clock and when I done it I banged against the
works and made the bell clang. So I jumped out of the
clock and tried it again, and done it better this time, at
least as good as I could without no training. Everybody
laughed.

But George Washington didn't see anything funny in
it. He went on staring at me grim and solemn, his
mouth straight as a ruler. I was covered with sweat and
wanted to wipe it away, but didn't dare for fear of

being rude. So in a low, whispery voice, I said, "I didn't mean nothing, sir," which wasn't much to say, but all I could think of with my head empty. I knew that Mr. Fraunces was there somewhere.

That got the President's tongue loose. "And what did you think you were doing in there?"

The truth was that I was spying, but I wasn't going to say that, for spying was a hanging offense. I needed a believable lie. Horace always said that the way to make a lie believable was to make yourself come out of it looking low and foolish. He said that if you told a lie that shined you up, nobody would believe it, even if it was true.

So I said, "Sir, them kitchen niggers told me that there was an owl in the clock who was trained to go whoo-whoo to tell the hours." Some of the ones standing around began to giggle, and that encouraged me to go on. "Well, I come out to oil the case like I always done, and my curiosity got going, and going, and blamed if I could help myself—I just had to see the owl."

Well, they just roared with laughter. I blushed, which I wasn't having no trouble doing anyways. The President, he didn't laugh, but went on staring at me with that mouth of his like a ruler, and the others shut up. Finally he said, "That's the stupidest thing I ever heard."

I began to wonder if I was making myself *too* low and foolish. But it was too late to go back, so I said, "I reckon it is, sir. It's about the stupidest thing I ever heard of, too."

91

"I'm glad to hear you admit it."

"Yes, sir," I said. "And just when I got inside and was looking around for the owl, everybody come in for dinner and I was stuck."

They all started giggling again. "Stuck?"

"Yes, sir," I said. "I dassn't come out because I wasn't dressed proper for no dinner party."

Well, they roared so they could hardly stand up. The men bent over and slapped themselves and laughed till they was like to bust, and the women roared, too, but behind their fans, because they was ladies, and not allowed to roar and slap themselves. Finally the President, he had to allow himself a smile. Then he waved his hand at me and said, "All right, go along."

"Yes, sir," I said, and I tore out of there lickety-split. But I knew that wasn't the end of it, for I was bound to hear about it from Mr. Fraunces. And after supper I did. Mr. Fraunces took me out into the back pantry and stood there staring at me mighty solemn, his mouth like a ruler, too. I blushed and looked down. "What in the name of heaven did you think you were doing, Carrie?"

I knew I was in trouble. It was all right to tell the President and the rest some story about owls, because they didn't know me and would believe I was that low and foolish. But Mr. Fraunces, he'd known me all my life, and he wasn't going to believe it, not for a minute.

"Did you really believe there was an owl in the clock, the way Mr. Lear says?"

I went on looking at the ground. "No, sir," I said.

"Then what were you doing?"

92

I went on looking at the ground. "I'll be honest, sir," which was the last thing I meant to be, "I wanted to see what was in there to make the hands go around."

I figured that would do it, because he knew me, and it did. "Someday that curiosity of yours is going to get you in a lot of trouble, Carrie."

"Yes, sir," I said. "I won't do it again."

Well, of course the story got all around, and for the next few days the kitchen help was all on me, asking if I knew what time it was, or if I was planning to go to President Washington's next dinner party, and such. But by and by it calmed down and they forgot about it.

But even after they forgot about it, every time I remembered, it made me feel down. I'd messed up my chance to talk to Dr. Johnson.

One day, around the middle of January, Mr. Fraunces come into the kitchen and gathered us all around. He told us he was going to leave the President's mansion. He said he was going back to his tavern. Because of the government having come to New York, business was so heavy his wife couldn't do it all herself and needed him back at the tavern, he said. We all knew that wasn't it. We knew it was all that fanciness and them extra wines and such that was moving him back to the tavern. Oh, I reckoned the other thing was true, too: business *was* mighty heavy in New York since the new government come. But the main reason was Mr. Fraunces got dismissed for extravagance.

And there went my last hope. It didn't matter anymore if President Washington moved to Philadelphia or Virginia or the moon. We was going back to the tavern, and I'd spend the rest of my life there washing pots and peeling potatoes. And I'd be lucky to do that, for Captain Ivers was sure to catch me sooner or later.

Oh, it was hard not having no choice about things and being at everybody's mercy, and not having no life of my own. I was at the bottom: there wasn't nobody lower than me, not even the tavern dogs. They could run off through the streets whenever they wanted to, or just lay around in front of the fire if they wanted to do that. They didn't work, neither, but got their food whether they done anything for it or not. It was hard being worse off than the dogs. Thinking about it, I near bust out crying in front of everybody; but I held it in until Mr. Fraunces left, and then I went out into the woodshed and cried for a while.

After a while I got tired of crying and stopped. Crying wasn't going to do me no good. Nobody was going to help me whether I cried a bucketful or went around laughing and singing all day long. The only person who would help me was myself. Oh, Dan, he'd help me if he could, and so would Mr. Fraunces, but that went only so far. The main person I had to count on was me. And suddenly I resolved that I *would* get out of my mess somehow. I *would* figure out a way somehow; and I wouldn't stop until I done it.

Thinking that cheered me up a good deal, and I wiped the tears off my face with my sleeve. Besides, it was cold out there in the woodshed. So I went back into the house carrying a load of wood, like that's

94

where I'd been, and when I'd dumped the logs in the wood box, I noticed a whole hot new apple tart on the pastry table that the cook had carelessly left where somebody could swipe it; and so as to prevent anybody from stealing it, I took it out to the pantry and ate it myself. It was the safest thing.

Anyway, Mr. Fraunces went back to the tavern, but he left me working for the President for a while. President Washington was moving to a different house, Mr. Fraunces said, and he needed extra help. Well, that was a relief to me, at least for now. For the more I thought about it, the more it seemed to me that I didn't have no choice but to run off. Once I was back at the tavern, Captain Ivers was bound to find out and come after me, and he'd catch me sooner or later. Oh, I didn't want to run away. I hated thinking about it. Mr. Fraunces had been good to me, and besides I was terrible scared to do it. But what else could I do?

The new steward was named Mr. Hyde. He come with his wife, who helped him to run things. They was all right, but I wasn't used to them. Mr. Fraunces treated me like family, but I wasn't family to the Hydes, and they would give me a cuff if I sassed anybody, instead of just a look the way Mr. Fraunces done.

The house the President chose to move into was supposed to be the grandest house in New York. It belonged to Count de Moustier, who was ambassador from France, and was going home. Some of us was sent over to clean the place and get it ready, and I had a chance to look it over. It was grand all right—four

95

stories high, with an attic on the top of that, and a big hall in the middle with stairs that wound up and up all the way to the top floor. If you went to the top you could lean over the rail and see all the way down to the bottom floor. My, it was scary standing way at the top of four flights of stairs and looking all the way down to the ground floor. But it was mighty grand.

Upstairs there was a balcony, with big glass doors all across the back, so's you could see over the orchards and fields clear to the North River. And just no end of big rooms.

The new house was only four or five blocks from Mr. Fraunces' tavern, and sometimes Horace stopped by to say hello if he happened to be out in that direction going to the market or taking a message for Mr. Fraunces. So I wasn't surprised when he come charging in one morning, while I was upstairs gleaming the windows that looked out toward the fields and the river. It was a dark day, with the clouds low and heavy, and I knew it was bound to snow soon. Horace stood at the bottom of the stairs looking up at the balconies and shouted, "Carrie?"

"I'm up here," I shouted back.

He panted up the stairs as fast as he could and didn't stop to catch his breath when he burst out, "Dan just come back from Philadelphia. He saw Willy. He says there's plenty of good jobs down there. I'm bound and determined to go." He was about as excited as I'd ever seen him, jigging around from one foot to the next, his eyes gleaming like candlelights.

96

I bit my lip to keep from crying. Here everybody was going off, and I was stuck for the rest of my life. "When are you going, Horace?" I tried to look happy for him, but he was so excited he wouldn't have noticed any way I looked.

"I ain't figured out yet. Soon, maybe. Dan says Captain Ivers is doing good business down in Philadelphia now. They'll be making a lot of trips. They're going right back down there tomorrow. Dan says he'll smuggle me on board when I'm ready. Captain Ivers don't go down into the hold, and if I sneak on board during the night I can hide down there among the cargo. It don't take more'n a day to get down to Philadelphia."

Suddenly, just like that, I decided I was going to Philadelphia, too. If Horace and Willy was going to be there, and Dan sailing in and out, I was determined I'd be there, too. I'd be sorry for leaving Mr. Fraunces. He raised me up and been kind to me. But I couldn't take a chance on going back to the tavern. I was bound I'd run off right then, and sail with the *Junius Brutus* the next day.

Horace went palavering on about what he would do when he got to Philadelphia, and how maybe he and Willy could get married and save their money, and start a tavern of their own. I wasn't listening, and by and by he said he had to go, and left.

I picked up the gleaming rag I'd dropped, but I didn't start gleaming with it. Instead I looked out the window. Already a few snowflakes was drifting down, just slow and lazy, zigzagging to the ground. It was

97

going to snow hard, that was for certain, and the *Junius Brutus* wasn't likely to leave in a heavy snowstorm. So unless they got off pretty soon, they would be stuck until the snow stopped. The way the clouds looked, we was in for a heavy snowfall that might last all day, and all night, too.

What was I going to do? I couldn't risk going back to the Cherry Street house that night. There was no telling where they might put me to work the next day, and I might not have a chance to skid off. I had to make a break for it pretty soon. There was four of us getting the new house ready for the President to move into. Old Will was in charge of us, but he usually started nipping at his rum in the morning, and by the middle of the afternoon he'd be snoozing somewhere. It wouldn't be no trouble to duck off.

Then what? The first thing would be to get down to the *Junius Brutus* and see if I could get ahold of Dan. I'd figure out the rest after that.

By early afternoon it was snowing pretty heavy, coming down quiet and soft and covering up the fields and the streets like poured cream. It was growing dark, too; you couldn't see more than fifty feet from the house. Once I was out there in that falling snow I'd get away, easy. So I bided my time, and went on gleaming windows. The afternoon dwindled away and the dark come on. We didn't have no lamps in the new house, and I knew we'd have to quit and go home pretty soon. I set down my rag, and went downstairs. One of the Mount

98

Vernon boys was down there, cleaning one of the fireplaces. "Where's old Will Lee?" I said.

"He's out by the kitchen fire, sleeping."

"Maybe you better wake him up so's we can go home," I said.

"Near dark, isn't it," he said. He got up from the fireplace and went out to the kitchen. I snatched up my cape from the banister where I'd left it, took a quick look around, and then slipped out of the house into the snow, my heart beating a mile a minute. I trotted off as quick as I could go, keeping my face down so's nobody who come along would recognize me. It was hard going: the snow was already halfway up to my knees. I tried to hold my skirt up so's it wouldn't get soaked, but it got wet anyway, and slapped around my legs like ice. It was slippery, too: twice I fell down.

But in five minutes I was out of sight of the house. I was pretty scared all right. They'd be looking for me already. A lot of black folks wouldn't tell on anybody that run off. The ones that were cleaning the new house wouldn't say anything—they'd just say that they didn't notice I was gone. But old Will Lee would. He was George Washington's favorite and he knew where his bread was buttered. Of course, there was a chance that he was drunk enough so's he would have forgotten how many people he took out with him that morning; but I couldn't count on it. I had to figure they was looking for me already.

# 11

IT WAS QUEER going along in the snowstorm—as quiet as could be with the lights from the houses on either side of me just yellow blurs. Every once in a while somebody would come along, or a horse slipping and sliding in the snow would come by pulling a wagon; but most everybody was at home.

To keep my mind off being scared and the wet skirt slapping at my legs, I let my curiosity run. Like, if I seen a girl my age through the window of some house, sitting by the fire sewing, I wondered what it was like to be white and free and sit home and sew instead of trotting around in the snow with my shoes wet and that dinged cold wet dress slapping at my legs. Or if I seen through a high window a chandelier dripping glass sparkling in candlelight, I'd try to guess what the room

100

was like, and who was in it—was there a party going on, or just a family sitting around with maybe the children eating cake while the father read them poems from out of a book. Or if I passed a confectioner's shop, with the windows just crammed full of fancy cakes and tarts and puddings and such, I would begin to wonder what this one or that one would taste like.

Finally I got to the waterfront. The ships was all lined up along the dock, their bowsprits pointing out over Water Street like branches of trees. Already the snow was beginning to pile up on them and on the yardarms and decks, so the ships was slowly turning white and soft. The lanterns on the decks made soft yellow spots in the falling snow.

I eased along, keeping close to the warehouses that lined the other side of the street. I was pretty sure I'd recognize the *Junius Brutus* when I saw it, because I'd seen it before, but I didn't want to take no chance of getting on the wrong ship. By and by I come to it. It was like the others, dressed in white, with a lantern sending off a thin yellow light somewhere near the stern.

I stood up against the warehouse, too scared and worried to think much about my wet shoes and my cold wet skirt clapped around my legs. What was I to do?

It didn't seem to me like I had much choice. I figured that Captain Ivers wouldn't be aboard—he'd be holed up in some tavern somewheres. And if he was on board he'd be below snug in his cabin, and wouldn't trouble himself to come up to see some little black girl.

So I crossed Water Street to where a plank come down from the deck of the *Junius Brutus*. It was covered with snow: nobody had been up or down it for hours. I started up it. It was slippery, and once my feet skidded out from under me and I near fell off it. It made a noise, and right away I saw the lantern at the stern begin to move up the deck toward me. I got to the top of the plank and waited, and in a minute there come the deck watch, carrying the lantern through the snow, so's that he was mostly a splotch of yellow.

"Who's there?" he said.

"I got a message for Dan Arabus. His Ma's mighty sick."

"He's down below," the watch said.

But I didn't want to go down there—I wouldn't have no chance to talk to him in the crew's quarters, with the sailors all around. "I'm too scared to climb down there," I said.

The watch held up the lantern to get a better look at me. "Scared, huh?" He sounded disgusted. He turned and went off with the lantern; and in about two minutes here came the lantern again through the snow. It was Dan. "Carrie," he said. "Who told you Ma's sick?"

I put my finger to my lips. "It ain't true. I was just saying that so's you'd come up."

"You shouldn't have done that, Carrie," he said. "It gave me a terrible scare."

"I couldn't help it, Dan." I grabbed him by the arm and sort of pulled him up toward the bow where we wasn't so close to the hatchway going down to

102

the crew's quarters. "Dan, are you going to Philadelphia?"

"Yes," he said. "We re supposed to sail in the morning, if the snow stops."

"Dan, I'm going to go with you. I'm going to run
away."

"What?"

"I got to go. I got to run away."

He took a look around, mighty worried. "Carrie, you
can't do that," he said in a low voice.

"I got to," I said. "You got to help me hide on board."

"You'll get into terrible trouble. If Ivers catches you,
he'll sell you off to the West Indies quick as he can." He
was still talking low.

"I got to chance it," I said.

He looked around again. "We can't talk about it
here." He beckoned me to follow, and we slipped down
the plank onto the dock, crossed Water Street, and
ducked down a little alley that went between two
warehouses. Dan knew all the ins and outs around
there. We crouched down out of the snow. I was beginning to feel good and cold. I kept brushing the snow
off me, but my skirt was wet and my shoes was wet, and
water kept leaking off my head and trickling down my
back, cold as could be.

"What took you so sudden about running away, Carrie?"

"It might be my only chance," I said. "I can't go back
to the tavern. Captain Ivers is bound to catch me there
sooner or later."

103

"Climbing on board his own ship ain't much of a way to get away from him."

"I got to risk it, Dan. It might be my only chance."

Suddenly I felt a sneeze coming on, tickling my nose. I put my hand over my face to muffle it, and then I sneezed.

"Carrie, you're getting sick already. You'll like to die hiding down in that hold for two days. There ain't any heat down there."

"You'll find me a blanket or a rag or a sail or something to wrap up in. I'll be all right."

"And you'd just run off and leave Mr. Fraunces like that?"

"Dan, remember when you was in trouble and you asked me go up to the wharf and see if the *Junius Brutus* was docked, and scout her out? And I done it, even though I risked being thrashed by the cooks?"

He stood there, looking at me. Then he said, "Well, all right, Carrie. But it's a mighty big risk."

Oh, I knew that all right. But I was resolved to do it. So we slipped back to the ship, and Dan went on up the plank while I waited down on the dock. In a minute he came back down. "The watch is at the stern. I'll go back up and slip the hatch cover open a little. You wait until you hear me say to the watch, 'Ain't that something out there in the water?' Then you come on board and climb down the hatchway into the hold. There's some barrels of molasses down there you can hide behind. Soon as I can, I'll try to bring you something to wrap up in."

Then he went back up the plank and disappeared in the falling snow. I crouched down by the plank and waited, feeling colder and colder, and shivering a good deal, too. In a minute I felt a sneeze coming on. I tried to hold it back; and I did for a bit, but then all of a sudden it broke loose. It was pretty loud and all I could hope was that nobody would think nothing of a sneeze in the snow.

Then I heard Dan say in a loud voice, "Ain't that something out there?" I slipped up the plank. It was good and dark, for Dan and the watch were at the stern of the ship, but I could make out shapes in the dark. I spotted the hatch cover, just a low blur. I slipped over to it and felt around it with my hands. Dan had shoved it part ways open. I reached down inside, found the ladder, swung over the hatch, and climbed down to the bottom.

There wasn't no light at all down there—not even a drop. I couldn't see my hand if I held it against my nose. I felt around, going most careful, because I didn't want to trip over nothing and make a noise. Finally I found the molasses casks and I sat down on one of them. In a couple of minutes I heard footsteps overhead and the hatch cover closed. I sat still, listening to the ship creak as it rolled in the water.

What worried me most was being cold and wet. I was awful feared of getting sick, and scared of sneezing, too. I took off my dress, rubbed myself dry as best I could and put the dress back on. It was still damp, but I figured my body heat would dry it off pretty soon.

105

It was a lot warmer inside the hold than outside, because there wasn't no wind, and no snow coming down. But there wasn't no heat in there, neither. I figured that the sailors had a little stove in their quarters, and Captain Ivers had one in the captain's quarters, too. But there wasn't one in the hold, and I could feel the chill stealing over me.

I began to feel around in the dark for a blanket or piece of sailcloth—anything that I could wrap up in. There was bound to be something. But I was scared of knocking something over and making a noise, and after a bit I gave it up. I'd best wait until Dan come with a lantern and helped me find something. So I sat and waited and dozed off a little, when I woke up I was shivering so hard I like to shake myself off the cask. My teeth was rattling, too, and hardly had I woke up when a sneeze come over me so fast I couldn't stop it. It just shot out; and another, and another. Then dead silence, except for the creaking of the ship.

My heart was racing. Them sneezes was as loud as explosions to me. It seemed like they must have blown the sailors right out of their beds. I heard a footstep going slowly overhead, and I thought surely the watch had heard them sneezes and was coming after me. But the footsteps went away down the deck.

I wished Dan would come with the light so's I could find something to get warm in and not sneeze no more. But he didn't come, and I figured he was stuck and couldn't get away. Or maybe he couldn't think of no excuse for coming down into the hold. I didn't know

106

what. I just wished he would come. So I sat there shivering and shaking and rattling my teeth and then here come the sneeze again. I wriggled my nose to make it go away, but it wouldn't. It kept coming and just in time I grabbed my nose and my mouth and covered them up. There was three of them, just like the last time, and they seemed like explosions again.

Still nobody come. I was about wore out with everything, and I lay down there on the casks, shivering and rattling, and by and by I fell asleep. I didn't sleep good. I dozed and come half awake and dozed again, and between times dreamed the most awful dreams that the devil was after me, all red with scaly skin and spouting fire out of his mouth, and his eyes red, too, like burning coals. Then I woke up. There was a bumping and creaking and slamming of things above, and the hatch cover was off and light streaming down. I felt just terrible—all hot and soaked in sweat and shaky, and I knew I was mighty sick.

Up on deck they was banging things around. I figured they was getting ready to sail. It wasn't snowing no more—at least there wasn't no snow coming down through the hatchway. The sun seemed pretty bright, and I figured it must be just after sunrise. I dropped down behind the casks where nobody could see me if they looked down the hatchway. I was too sick to worry much about anything. I wasn't thinking about who I was or anything. I just wanted to lie there and not move and not have nothing trouble me. Then I felt a sneeze come over me and there wasn't nothing I could

107

do about it, and I didn't care no more, neither. So I sneezed and went on sneezing a few more times and then I heard a voice say, "Somebody's down there. Who's down there?" I looked up at the hatchway. Somebody was crouched over it, looking down. It was one of the sailors, I reckoned. After a minute he stood up and said to somebody I couldn't see, "I swear somebody's down there."

Then I heard Dan say, "I'll go look." He come in sight over the hatchway and climbed down the ladder. He wound his way through the casks and boxes toward me and when he got to where I was lying there sweating and shaking he looked back at the hatch. "I don't see nobody, sir."

"Well, have a good look. I swear I heard somebody."

So Dan gave me a wink and wound around through the boxes and such, and then wound his way back to me. "You don't look good, Carrie," he whispered.

I couldn't hardly talk. I just shook my head.

He took a quick look back at the hatch to see if anyone was watching. Nobody was. He knelt down beside me and felt my forehead. "You're hot as fire, Carrie. I reckon you're pretty sick."

"I reckon I am," I said.

"I don't think you ought to go with us," he said. He looked worried as could be.

"It's too late, Dan," I whispered. "I can't go back. I got to risk it."

Then a big voice come from above. "Who're you talking to down there?"

Dan stood up. "I ain't—" he started to say, but here come some man down the ladder. He wound his way over to us. If Dan hadn't been there, he might not have seen me lying behind the cask, but he headed straight for Dan and in a minute he was standing over me. I closed my eyes.

"Who's this nigger?"

"She's mighty sick, mate," Dan said.

"I can see that," the mate said. "How'd she come here?"

"I know her," Dan said. "She must have followed me along and crept on board last night when nobody was looking."

The mate looked down at me. "Come on now," he said. "On your feet."

I sat up slowly. "I ain't got no strength, sir," I kind of whispered.

"I don't want you sick on this ship," the mate said. "You'll spread it to everybody."

Dan grabbed my arm and helped me up. I made it over to the ladder and started up, feeling just terrible. I climbed up the ladder with Dan boosting me along from behind, and climbed over the top. Like I figured, the sun was just coming up over Brooklyn, and shining bright as fire off the snow. There was so much light I could see ships miles down the harbor just as sharp as could be.

Some sailors was standing around watching. Two of them was black and I wondered if they was slaves like Dan, or free sailors who was earning their own money.

109

I stood there shaking and shivering, and here come Captain Ivers.

Captain Ivers stared at me, his face so cold and still. I could see he didn't recognize me: white folks was like that. Finally he said, "Where did you come from? Speak up."

I wasn't about to say nothing about Fraunces Tavern. "I work at the President's mansion."

He stared at me some more. "I've seen you before. Where have I seen you before?"

"I don't know, sir. I don't think so, sir."

He reached and grabbed a chunk of my hair and give it a tug. "Don't contradict me," he said. "If I say I've seen you before, I've seen you before. Where was it?" He went on holding onto my hair.

"I don't know, sir," I said.

He gave my hair a tug. "Answer," he said. "Tell the truth or I'll beat it out of you."

"Please, sir, I work at the President's mansion."

"The President's—Sam Fraunces—that's it," he said. "You're the nigger girl from Fraunces Tavern." And the corners of his mouth raised up into a tiny smile. "*My* nigger girl now." He turned to the mate. "Have somebody take her below and tie her to something. And wrap her up in something so she don't die on us. I don't want any dead niggers on my ship."

He started to turn away, but Dan touched his arm and said, "Sir, it's true. She's one of President Washington's house niggers."

Captain Ivers stopped dead in his tracks and swiveled

around. He stared at me with that cold face, and then at Dan and then back to me. "Is that the truth?"

"Yes, sir," I whispered. "I been working for him since he come to New York."

He turned his head and stared out into the harbor, his face still as ice. He knew he dassn't steal a slave from the President of the United States. He wouldn't dare do that no matter how much money I was worth.

He swung back, grabbed the front of my dress, and shook me. "You sure you're not lying?"

"No, sir, I ain't lying," I said.

"It's the truth," Dan said. "You can carry her back over there and find out, sir. I reckon the President would be powerful glad if somebody brought back a runaway slave to him."

Sick as I was, I seen how smart that was. Captain Ivers turned to stare out in the harbor again. Then he looked at Dan and looked at me and said, "I'm going to see for myself, mate," he said. "Make the ship ready. We'll sail the minute I get back."

Well, I was in for trouble. I done too many things wrong, and now with running away they was likely to do something serious. But I was too sick to care.

# 12

CAPTAIN IVERS was in an all-fired rush. He pushed me down the plank and along Water Street toward the President's mansion. Being as it was early in the morning there hadn't been much traffic through, and the snow was deep and the streets near empty of people. It was so bright it hurt my eyes. Captain Ivers kept pushing me along and I kept stumbling. Finally we was at the President's mansion.

Captain Ivers didn't go around to the kitchen door the way I would have done, but marched right up to the front door. One of the stableboys was already shoveling the snow off the steps. Captain Ivers stepped right up and rang the bell. In a minute Mr. Lear swung the door open. He looked pretty puzzled to see us standing there.

"I'm Captain Thomas Ivers. I found this nigger wench on my ship. She tells me she's one of yours."

Mr. Lear looked at me. "Yes, I think she is," he said. "I'll get the steward."

Captain Ivers stepped up to go inside but Mr. Lear shut the door and he was left outside.

In a minute he came back with Mr. Hyde. "This wench says she's one of yours," Captain Ivers said.

"That's right," Mr. Hyde said. "But as far as I'm concerned she can go back to Sam Fraunces. She's more trouble than she's worth."

Captain Ivers' mouth tipped up again in that tiny smile.

"Well, sir," Captain Ivers said. "In that case I'll just take her around to Fraunces." But I knew there was no way he was going to take me back to the tavern. He would march me right back to the ship and sell me off to the West Indies. I was done for. He spun me around, and started to push me off down into the street, when just then we heard a commotion behind us. Captain Ivers turned around to look, and so did I.

Mr. Lear was standing in the doorway, with the President right behind him. The secretary had on his overcoat and hat. "Let me know immediately how Jefferson responds to the idea," the President said.

Captain Ivers pushed me out of the way. The secretary come down the steps and went off, and then President Washington noticed us standing in the snow. "What's this?" he said.

Captain Ivers bowed. "Good morning, Your Excel-

113

lency," he said, doing his best to work up a smile. "I found this wench stowed away aboard my ship. I brought her back, but it turns out she belongs to Sam Fraunces."

The President stared down at us, mighty solemn. Then he said, "Why, it's the little wench from the clock." He looked at me careful. "She looks ill."

"She was clearly trying to run away." Captain Ivers was still working on the smile, but he hadn't much practice at it, and it kept flickering and going out. "She claims she belongs here, but the steward says she belongs to Sam Fraunces."

The President looked me over some more in his serious way. "She certainly did belong here at one time," he said. "I'm not surprised you found her on your ship. She has a way of turning up in odd places."

Captain Ivers bowed again. "If she's not yours, Your Excellency, I'll take her around to Sam Fraunces."

"I'm not sure about that," President Washington said. "She's sick in any case. She shouldn't be traipsing around in the snow. Mr. Hyde, put her to bed. We can't send her back to Sam sick." Then he went back into the house and shut the door behind him.

The ice on Captain Ivers' face crackled like somebody had hit it with a heavy stone. But he dassn't go against the President. He swiveled around and marched off to the ship, and Mr. Hyde took me around to the kitchen door and brought me inside. The warmth flooded around me and I was so grateful to be out of

114

the snow the tears just leaked out of my eyes and run down my face in buckets.

The Hydes fixed me up a heap of blankets in the laundry room near the stove and give me some soup to drink, which was about all I could manage anyway, and I dozed and woke up covered with sweat and dozed some more and didn't know nothing about what was going on except that every once in a while one of the Mount Vernon boys was shoving some soup at me.

I was sick like that for three or four days. Finally my fever went down and I began to feel a little better— weak and tired, but taking a little interest in what was going on around me. A couple of more days and I was taking an interest in food as well; and once the Hydes saw that I could stuff in a chunk of pork and a half a loaf of bread without no trouble, they figured I was well enough to do a little work, and they set me going in the kitchen again. And I was sitting there in the kitchen peeling potatoes one day when Mr. Fraunces turned up. We started back to the tavern, walking through the slush and snow. "Now what's this all about, Carrie—running away and all that?"

So I told him the whole story—how I was terrible scared of going back to the tavern, for fear that Captain Ivers would catch me and sell me off to the West Indies. And Willy'd gone to Philadelphia, and Horace was going, and Dan visiting there all the time, too, and I wouldn't have nobody left at the tavern. And on top of it, I didn't know who I was, and didn't have no last

115

name and none of that. Just telling it made me so sad the tears started to trickle out.

Mr. Fraunces he just listened and nodded, and finally said, "It would help if we could find out more about where you came from. We might find out if Ivers has any real claim on you."

"Yes, sir," I said. "It's mighty hard not knowing who you are."

"I think I'd better see Dr. Johnson. I'll do it soon."

Well, that lifted me up. I quit crying and wiped my eyes and said, "Oh, thank you, sir."

"I'll see to it right away, Carrie. In the meantime, you keep a sharp eye out for Ivers."

Even so, I was glad to be back at the tavern again. Oh, working at the President's mansion was full of glory, that was true, and I was proud of it, and would always, all the rest of my life, tell people I'd done it, and spoken to George Washington himself, and got his spit on me from washing his dishes and all that.

But to be honest, it was a whole lot easier at the tavern. We didn't have so much gleaming to do at the tavern as we did at the President's, and we didn't have to be so careful about watching our manners, and not cursing, and doing everything just so. Oh, Mr. Fraunces had his rules: we had to be polite and do what we was told and not sass the guests. But it was lax.

Horace, he was glad to have me back. Partly it was out of friendship, and partly because he missed having someone lower than him around. But part of it was because it hurt him so to be at the tavern when I was

over at President Washington's gleaming things. It
made him feel much better that I was back. "I don't
mean nothing by it, Carrie," he said, "but I knew you
wasn't cut out for it. You ain't had the experience. You
ain't done nothing but peel potatoes and pump water
all your life, where I spent years doing near everything
you can do in a dining room. I grew up with it, nearly,
and there ain't nothing anyone can tell me about it."

"Oh, I believe that," I said. "There ain't much anybody can tell you about anything, Horace. I reckon you
could give President Washington himself lessons in it."

"You better watch how you sass people, Carrie," he
said. "I ain't going to stand for it much longer."

"Well, sit then." He took a snap at me with his polish-
ing rag, but I ducked.

A week went by and another week, and every few
days Mr. Fraunces would say, "I haven't forgotten
about Dr. Johnson, Carrie." But nothing happened
about it.

Then finally one morning after breakfast Mr.
Fraunces came out to the kitchen and told me come
down to his office. I followed him down the hall and
there sitting in a chair next to Mr. Fraunces' desk was
Dr. Johnson. I recognized him without no trouble:
everything that happened that time the President
caught me in his clock was stuck tight in my head.

He looked at me sort of puzzled. "I've seen you before," he said.

I blushed. "Yes, sir," I said. "I was the girl in the
clock."

117

He laughed. "That was you, was it?"

"I didn't mean nothing by it, sir."

"I don't think anyone was angry at you," he said. "I think they were rather amused."

Mr. Fraunces sat down behind his desk, and I stood there on the fancy carpet, facing them. "Now—what's your name again?" Dr. Johnson said.

"Carrie, sir. I don't have no last name."

He nodded. "Sam says you're curious about your background."

"Yes, sir," I said. "It's mighty hard not knowing who you are or where you come from."

He thought about that for a minute. "I suppose it would be," he said. "Well, I'm not sure how much help I can be. But I'll tell you what I can."

"Yes, sir," I said.

"The main clue we have is that Jack Arabus brought you here. I remember drawing up some papers for Jack, but it was a long time ago and I don't remember just what they were. I looked through all my papers that pertained to Jack Arabus and I didn't find anything. But while I was doing that something came back to me."

"Yes, sir," I said.

"I remember Jack being concerned about a child he'd picked up somewhere. He had a paper which he showed to me. The child had been born somewhere around New York while the British troops were occupying the city. It might have been on Staten Island. It makes sense that it was Staten Island, anyway, because

118

Jack was with Washington's army in New Jersey, and it would have been easy enough for him to slip onto Staten Island and visit somebody there. Nobody would have paid any attention to a black man if he wasn't wearing a uniform."

"And he found a child there, sir?"

"Well, he didn't exactly find the child, I guess. As I remember, the mother was working for the British troops there, doing laundry or kitchen work or something of the kind. And for some reason she couldn't keep the child. I just don't know. Anyway, Jack seems to have taken the child, and along with her he got a paper signed by a British officer out there. That was why Jack came to me. He wanted me to look over the paper and see if it was legal."

"And was it, sir?" I said.

"Yes, as I remember. It was some kind of an informal birth certificate. I think the point of it was that the woman was free, and she wanted to be sure the child was free, too."

"Free?" I kind of gasped out. "And it was me?"

Now Mr. Fraunces held up his hand. "Carrie, don't get too excited about this. We don't know if you and the child are the same person. It seems likely, but there's nothing here that would hold up in court."

"Mr. Fraunces is right, Carrie," Dr. Johnson said. "We don't know who that child was. Of course, it seems reasonable to suppose that you are that child. We can guess that for some reason Jack had responsibility for the child. Of course, he couldn't have taken care of a child while he was in the army and he left it with Sam Fraunces."

"We know at least that Jack left you here, Carrie," Mr. Fraunces said.

"It has to be me, sir," I said. But I was so excited I could hardly talk. "Who else could it be?" What I didn't say was that it meant I was free. I could hardly believe it. I didn't dare to believe it, either, for fear that it wasn't true. "How can I find out more, sir?" I blurted out.

Dr. Johnson shook his head. "I don't know. We don't know where that paper is. I never even knew what had become of that child. I'd forgotten all about the whole thing. Jack's been dead for four years. There's no telling what he did with the paper."

I was excited, but mighty confused. "Sir, that's all you know about me?"

Dr. Johnson nodded. "I'm afraid so, Carrie. It was a long time ago, the Revolution was still being fought, and families were being disrupted everywhere. The story was common enough, and I didn't give it much thought. It was just one more child orphaned in the confusions of war."

"But I might be free, sir."

Mr. Fraunces shook his head. "Carrie, we won't know that until we find out exactly who you are. Remember, Ivers is still pressing his claim to you. If he catches you, it won't matter what we find out about you."

"It isn't fair, sir," I cried. "It isn't fair."

The men didn't say nothing. They just looked at each

120

other. Finally Mr. Fraunces said in a soft voice, "No, Carrie, it isn't fair. It isn't fair that anybody should be a slave. At the time the Constitution was being written three years ago a lot of us hoped that slavery would be abolished in the United States. It could have been done gradually."

Dr. Johnson broke in, "But in the South, Sam, too much depends on slave labor. Down there the money comes from big plantations—rice and indigo and tobacco. The farmers there were afraid that if their slaves were taken away from them the whole economic system of the area would collapse. Most of them were, anyway. There were some who thought the South would be better off without slavery. But they were a small minority. And so we still have slavery in the United States."

"But, sir," I said. "They don't have it in Massachusetts no more."

"That's true," Dr. Johnson said. "They've got rid of it there, and the chances are that most of the northern states will abolish slavery in a few years. But that doesn't do you much good now, does it?"

"No, sir," I said. I was feeling sad all over again. There didn't seem no way out. There was one question I wanted to ask, though. I knew I shouldn't; but I had to anyway. "Mr. Fraunces, you could free me, couldn't you?"

Mr. Fraunces stared at me for a minute. Then he said, "Carrie, I don't own you. All I know about you for certain is that Jack Arabus brought you here. I don't

121

know whether you were free or slave or what. From what Dr. Johnson said, it appears that you might have been free-born. But we don't know that for sure." He stopped for a minute to think. Then he said, "There's something else, too. As long as it seems that you're my slave, there's less chance of your being kidnapped by Ivers, or somebody else. It's one thing to kidnap a free black; it's another to steal a man's property. That's why I've always let it seem that you were my slave. It was safer that way. But legally you aren't my slave."

Then nobody said nothing. Dr. Johnson got up, and Mr. Fraunces did, too. I made a curtsy, the best one I knew how, anyway. I felt mighty low and miserable. "Thank you, sir," I said. And I stepped out of the way to let Dr. Johnson leave.

But he didn't. He stood there staring at me for a minute. Then he said, "I just remembered something else. I don't know what importance it has, but Colonel Ledyard had something to do with it. I distinctly remember Jack Arabus mentioning his name. I was struck by it at the time, because Ledyard was quite a well-known man around Connecticut."

"Ledyard?" Mr. Fraunces said. "The name's familiar."

"He was well known during the Revolution. He was killed in the massacre at Groton. It was in the newspapers at the time."

Mr. Fraunces nodded. "That must be where I heard the name. It was some time ago."

"Sir, what did Colonel Ledyard have to do with me, sir?"

122

Dr. Johnson shook his head. "I don't know. Perhaps nothing. I just remember Jack Arabus bringing the name up at the time."

Then nobody said nothing. I made my little curtsy again, and Dr. Johnson left. He was a mighty important man and didn't have too much time for someone as low as me.

# 13

I WENT BACK to the kitchen and got to work on a heap
of potatoes, but my mind wasn't on them. It just kept
wandering around restless, like a lost dog that's almost
got home but can't find the rest of the way. My mind
just prowled along one street and down another and
then turned around and come back and tried a back
alley to see where it come out. But it didn't come out
anywhere. I couldn't make anything out of it. All I
knew was that until I could prove who I was, I was
stuck. And I might be stuck anyway, if Captain Ivers
got his way in court.

But I wasn't the only one who was stuck. Horace was
the next one. Word began to come around that the
Hydes wasn't doing no better than Mr. Fraunces did at
the President's mansion. It turned out they was even

more extravagant, serving six or seven wines instead of four or five and giving the left-over bottles to the servants, so they was drunk half the time. Finally Mr. Lear fired a couple of them for drinking. Well, the Hydes was mighty upset and they come to Mr. Fraunces and asked what they should do. Mr. Fraunces felt sorry for them, even though they'd taken his old job. He said he would send over to them one of his waiters who didn't drink and knew all about setting up a dining room. That was Horace.

Well Horace, he was fit to be tied. Here he'd got it all worked out that he was going to leave Fraunces Tavern and go down to Philadelphia to work with Willy.

But now he was to go to work at the President's mansion. Oh, he was hot and bothered. You couldn't just quit working for the President the way you could quit Fraunces Tavern. If the President wanted you to work in his house, why that was where you worked, and nothing more said about it. Once he got there, he would be stuck. He told Mr. Fraunces he wasn't sure he ought to go, things was bound to go wrong at the tavern if he wasn't around to see to things, and probably it would just set up jealousy with the Mount Vernon help since Horace was such a prince at laying out a dining room and knew more about it than they did. But Mr. Fraunces said no, Horace deserved the chance, and that Horace wasn't to worry about the tavern, Mrs. Fraunces would see to things. So along about the middle of June he went, carrying his things in a sack over his shoulder, looking mighty gloomy.

On top of it, Dan didn't turn up the way he usually did. Horace was mighty fretful about that, too, for Dan was to have been in Philadelphia, and most likely would see Willy, and Horace was mighty anxious to get word from her. "Ding President Washington," he said. "I might just skid off to Philadelphia on the *Junius Brutus* anyway, next time Dan goes there."

I got over to see Horace as frequent as I could. Luckily there was plenty of excuses for it, for there was always a lot of messages going back and forth between Mr. Fraunces and the Hydes, and like as not I'd carry them. But it wasn't the same as having Horace right there where I could get at him whenever I had the need to sass somebody.

March passed, and the snow melted, and spring begun to come. We was glad to see it, as we always was. Winters was hard. The streets was always mushy and wet and when it was cold and the wind blew, there wasn't no way you could keep the tavern warm no matter how much wood you chunked on the fire. The only way to stay warm was to sit close to the fire, and when you was the lowest person around, you was always farthest from the fire.

So I was glad to see April and then here comes May, with the trees going yellowy green with buds, like they was growing light green fur, the sun warm and the grass in the yard smelling new and sweet. And suddenly one evening as I was sitting out back after dinner, resting and cooling myself off, Dan come down the

126

alley beside the tavern, whistling to himself. I jumped up and run to him and he give me a big hug. "Where you been, Dan?" I said. "Horace has nearly fret himself to death. He ain't but skin and bones."

"We went down to the West Indies. 'Stacia. We was down there a considerable time, and then we came back to Philadelphia, and up to Connecticut and we ain't been back to New York since." He stepped back and looked at me. "Well, you seem all right. That last time I saw you, you was near to dying. I was mighty worried."

"You was worried, Dan?"

He give me a look. "Not that worried. I figured you're pretty tough and not easy to kill."

"Still, you was worried."

He didn't answer that. "Where's Horace? I saw Willy both times I was in Philadelphia."

"He don't work here anymore," I said. "He works over at the President's mansion now."

"He must be mighty set up about that."

"He ain't. He was all set on going down to Philadelphia to marry Willy, and now he's stuck."

"I don't know as he ought to be so set on marrying Willy. She told me to tell Horace that there was plenty of good jobs for waiters down in Philadelphia, but for him not to be so fired up about getting married. She hasn't made up her mind. But he could come down if he wants."

"He ain't going to like that too much," I said.

"Well," Dan said, "there's a lot of talk about the government moving to Philadelphia. Maybe he'll get there, anyway."

"They was talking like that a year ago," I said.

"Yes, but this time it's more serious. Leastwise that's what the talk is in Philadelphia."

I got Dan something to eat and we set outside listening to the peepers go, and smelling the spring smells all around. It was just like the old days, and it made me happy just to be setting there with him, watching him eat and listening to him talk. He told me about 'Stacia, and the things they saw there, and after a while he got onto the subject of his notes, like he always done.

There was trouble about them again. "The House of Representatives has voted not to pay off on the state notes. But that ain't the last word on it. They're only one part of Congress and the whole Congress has got to decide. There's still a chance that they'll pay off the United States notes, which is mostly what I got. But it was mighty disappointing to everybody who has the notes, and the prices has gone off something awful. I can't take a chance on it no more. I got to sell."

"But suppose the Congress votes for them—they'll be worth a whole lot more."

"Yes, but if they vote against them, the way the House of Representatives just did against the state notes, they won't be worth anything at all. Just paper, that's what they'd be, and you may as well wrap your dinner in them."

I thought about that. "It don't seem fair, Dan. I mean your daddy fought in the war and risked his life for

128

that money and now it ain't going to be worth nothing."

"Well, he got his freedom, too," Dan said. "That was what he was really fighting for. He figured on using the money to buy me and Ma free, too."

"But he drowned and didn't get no benefit from it." Suddenly something come to me. "Dan, I wonder if my daddy got any notes, so as to buy me free."

Dan thought about that for a minute. "Well," he said, "if he fought in the Revolution he would have got free on account of that. All the blacks that fought got free. My daddy's court case proved that they had to be set free, no matter what their old master said. Leastwise, in Connecticut. And he'd have been paid notes, too. But he might have sold them. Or he might have got killed before he was paid them. Being as you don't know who your daddy was, it doesn't matter one way or another."

"Still," I said, "maybe he was planning on buying me free, if he wasn't killed."

Dan shrugged. "Maybe they ain't going to be worth anything, anyway."

"It's not fair," I said.

"No, it ain't," Dan said. "But some of the states has already paid off their notes, and they figure that they shouldn't be taxed by the United States government to pay off the other states' notes."

I could see the point of that. "What are you going to do, Dan?"

"I'm going to sell. I'm going to see Dr. Johnson and ask him to sell the notes for me for whatever he can get."

"Is it enough to buy you free, Dan?"

He shook his head. "I don't aim to buy myself free. I aim to buy Ma free."

Well, that shook me some. "Buy your Ma free? But what about you, Dan?"

He looked around to see that nobody was listening. "Don't tell nobody," he whispered. "Don't even tell Horace. I'm going to buy Ma free, and then I'm going to run away."

It was all so unexpected it made me feel dizzy, like I spun around too fast. "Where are you going to run off to?"

He looked around again to make sure no one was listening. "Boston, Massachusetts, most likely. Captain Ivers don't go there too frequent, and slavery ain't allowed. I could set up as a fisherman, like my Pa did in Connecticut."

It was all I could do to keep from crying. I felt just sick. "Couldn't you run away to New York, Dan?"

"Not a chance of it," he said. "Too many people down here know me, especially around the waterfront. Captain Ivers would advertise for me. He'd put up handbills with my picture on it, and such. He did that once before. Anybody who saw me would turn me in for the reward. Besides, slavery's still legal here. And then there's all these kidnappers. I wouldn't last a minute in New York."

Then I did bust out crying. I couldn't help myself. I felt so mixed up. Everything inside of me was coming and going this way and that. He was running off from

130

me, too, and that made me sick and mad at him, and sorry for myself.

But I didn't want Dan to know I was crying over him. He wasn't the kind that liked having nobody cry over him. I was so confused I couldn't stand it no more. I jumped up and run off into the barn and hid behind some hay. I heard Dan say, "Carrie?" In a moment I seen his shape standing at the barn door, the tavern lights behind him and the stars over his head, and I loved him so much I thought I'd die. The tears run down my face and I shook and shook from trying not to make no noise.

He stood there and called my name. "Carrie. What's the matter, Carrie?" Still I didn't answer. And finally he trudged off down the alley by the tavern. I wanted to get up and run after him and tell him I loved him and he mustn't go away or I'd die. But I didn't.

Well, I was down near to the bottom. I'd come to a dead end on finding out who I was, and I'd lost Dan, and Horace wasn't around no more. It had all gone wrong somehow, and it didn't seem like there was anything I could do about it. Oh, how I wished I'd run out of the barn and told Dan I didn't mean to cry, and all that; but it was too late.

The days went by, and I felt like all the life was sucked out of me. I didn't have no interest in anything.

If I saw a piece of pie laying on a table, just begging to be stole, I'd like as not leave it lay as take it. Or if the cooks was all off somewheres, and there wasn't nothing to keep me from skidding off to the haymow for a snooze, why chances were I'd just go on peeling potatoes or whatever I was supposed to be doing. Nothing mattered to me anymore. I even lost my curiosity. Once they was to send up a big balloon with folks riding in a basket only three blocks away from the tavern. I could have skidded off easy, which everybody else done; but it didn't seem worth the trouble.

About four days later Horace come over to the tavern. I was out in the barn, where I was supposed to be collecting eggs, just setting there in a barrow, feeling low and not caring about anything, listening to the chickens cluck and smelling the hay and dust.

Horace come out and stood there looking at me. "What's the matter, Carrie?"

"Nothing," I said.

"There is too," he said.

But I didn't want to tell him about Dan, so I said, "It just don't look like I'm ever going to find out who I am."

"Since you can't do nothing about it, there ain't no sense in fretting," he said. "Try to think of something else."

I felt too low to argue with him about it. I gave him a look, but I didn't say nothing.

He went on standing in front of me. "Did Mr. Fraunces ever take you to see Dr. Johnson?"

"He come up here to see me," I said.

"He wasn't no help?"

"Not much," I said. "He said Jack Arabus got a

132

child from some woman who was working for the British soldiers out on Staten Island, and maybe that's who I was. Dr. Johnson, he didn't have any papers on it, and it didn't prove nothing."

"That's all he knew?"

"He said that Jack Arabus had some paper saying that I was free—leastwise, my ma was—but Jack Arabus is dead and nobody knows where the paper is."

"Free?" Horace said. "Why, that's wonderful, Carrie."

"No it ain't," I said. "I can't prove it, and anyway, if Captain Ivers catches up to me he'll claim I was his slave all along and it won't matter what anybody says if they can't prove nothing about me."

"Well, it's something anyway, Carrie." He was trying to cheer me up. "At least you know you was born."

I gave him a look. "I always reckoned I was."

"No, I mean where you were born," he said.

"It ain't much. I still don't know who my Ma was or my Pa."

"That's all Dr. Johnson said?"

"That's all he knew about it," I said. "Oh, and he said something about Colonel Ledyard that was involved in it, but he didn't know how."

Horace gave me a funny look. "Colonel Ledyard?"

"Or something," I said. "I couldn't make no sense out of it."

Horace went on staring at me. "The Ledyards from Groton, Connecticut?"

"From up there somewheres," I said.

"Why ding it, Carrie, Colonel Ledyard was Willy

Freeman's old master, that freed them when Willy's Pa
joined up with the militia to fight."

My heart began to beat so I could hear it. I knew I
was on to something. I didn't know what exactly, but
that poor lost dog had got a sniff of home, and knew it
was just around a corner somewhere, if he could only
find the right corner. "Horace," I said, "what do you
make of it?"

"I'm dinged if I know," he said. "You didn't never
belong to Colonel Ledyard. You wasn't ever up in
Groton."

That smell of home was getting stronger. "Tell me
about Willy's mother some more," I said.

"Why there ain't much to tell. She got captured by
the British after the fighting at Groton, where Willy
saw her Pa get run through with a sword."

"And then what happened?"

"She got hauled off to New York, where the British
was holed up. Then when the Revolution was over and
the British sailed away, they turned her loose. She was
mighty sick, and she went up to Stratford to stay at
Captain Ivers' house with Dan's mother, and she died."

"Why did she go up to stay with Dan's mother?"

"Dan's mother was her sister. You know that, Carrie.
Dan is Willy's cousin."

That lost dog was near home—I knew what it was.
"And Jack Arabus was Dan's daddy. So he was kin to
Willy's mother."

"Why, Carrie, what are you going on this way for,"

134

Horace said. "Jack Arabus was Willy's uncle. Everybody knows that."

I was plenty excited, just sparkling inside as bright as could be. "So if Willy's mother had a little baby while she was a prisoner of the British, who would she hand the baby over to?"

Well, Horace, he didn't say anything. He stared at me, and then he looked down at the dust and pieces of hay on the ground, and then he looked back at me, frowning. "I don't see what you're getting at, Carrie."

"It's as plain as day, Horace," I said.

"It isn't plain to me."

"Well, it is to me. Willy's mother was my mother, too. I'm Willy's sister."

"No," Horace said. "You're just making it up."

But it didn't bother me none what he thought. I knew I was right. It was the only thing that made sense. "Yes I am," I said. "I'm Willy's sister all right." What a feeling it gave me all of a sudden to know who my Ma and Pa was. Oh, there wasn't no feeling in the world like that. Just like that I wasn't nobody no more. I was somebody, and maybe free, too. Oh, there wasn't no feeling like it.

Horace shook his head, mighty solemn. I could tell that he didn't like the idea of anybody else having a claim on Willy. "No, I can't see it, Carrie. Willy never said nothing about it."

"That don't matter," I said. "It's the only thing that makes sense. See if Mr. Fraunces don't agree."

# 14

It took me a whole day before Mr. Fraunces had time to see me. After supper we went down to his office and I stood on that fancy carpet next to his shiny desk, hearing the peepers outside, and smelling the spring flowers. "What is it, Carrie?" he said.

"Sir, I figured out who I am."

"You did?"

"Yes, sir," I said. "I'm Willy Freeman's sister. I never was nobody's slave."

He jerked his head up and stared at me, and then he said, "By the Lord, there is a resemblance. How did you figure that?"

"Horace told me about Colonel Ledyard. He was Willy's Pa's old master, that set them all free when Willy's Pa joined the army."

Mr. Fraunces frowned, and tapped his fingers on his desk. "Colonel Ledyard. I knew there was something familiar about that name. Of course, that's right. He was Willy's old master. He manumitted the family when Jordan Freeman joined the militia."

"Yes, sir," I said. "It means I'm free."

Mr. Fraunces held up his hand the way he always did. "Just a minute, Carrie," he said. He sat there thinking for a while. Then he said, "All right, explain it."

"It just has to be, sir. Why else would that woman have given the child to Jack Arabus?"

He nodded. "That certainly makes sense. Willy's mother was being held by the British somewhere around New York. I remember Willy telling me that. And if she'd had a baby, Jack would have been the logical person to have given it to."

My eyes was so bright I could just feel them shining. "And Jack Arabus, he couldn't keep no baby in the army, so he brought me here to you."

He sat there thinking and tapping and then he said, "Yes, Carrie, it's plausible. It fits together. But there are a lot of pieces missing. Why didn't Jack say anything to me about who you were? Why didn't Willy know of your existence? Or Dan. His mother was your mother's sister—if that's who she was—and she certainly would have told her sister she'd had a child. Why didn't Dan know?"

"I don't know, sir," I said. "But I know who I am. I'm Willy's sister."

He smiled. Then he said, "I hope it's true, Carrie. It

would certainly be nice for you. But you'll need more than just a lot of stories to prove in court that you're free if Captain Ivers catches you."

"I know that, sir," I said. "But I'll find a way."

But when I thought about it later, out in the yard filling the water buckets, I wasn't so sure about it. Mr. Fraunces was right. It was clear enough to me who I was, but I didn't have no papers on it. If I could find that paper Jack Arabus had showed to Dr. Johnson it would be a help, but I still couldn't prove it was me the paper was talking about. I knew who I was all right; but if even Horace didn't believe me, it wasn't going to be easy to get anybody else to believe me.

It come on June and the trees was in full bloom and the weather warm and nice, but all I could feel was itchy. I wasn't sure of nothing anymore. The person I wanted to talk to most of all was Dan. He was smart, he'd have ideas about it. But I wasn't sure if he was mad at me for busting into tears in front of him and hiding on him. I wished he'd come so I could tell him I was sorry for what I'd done, and wouldn't hide on him no more. 'Course, there was a problem about Dan. Willy was Dan's cousin, and if I was Willy's sister, Dan was my cousin, too. I began to wonder if it was right to have such loving feelings for a cousin. It bothered me some, but I thought I'd wait to see if it made any difference next time I saw him.

And then one morning Horace come around with a message from the Hydes for Mr. Fraunces about whether George Washington liked his sausages boiled or fried. He come in through the kitchen and give me a wink and went through to see Mr. Fraunces.

About five minutes later he come back through the kitchen and give me another wink and went out into the kitchen yard, and I skidded off after him.

"Where you going, Nosey?" the third cook said.

"Don't call me Nosey," I said. Oh, would it be a great day when I could tell them cooks I was free and had a last name and didn't have to put up with their bossiness all the time.

I went out into the yard. Horace was waiting by the pump. "Dan's in New York," he said. "He came around to the President's mansion last night."

"Oh," I said. It was mighty hurtful that he didn't come and see me.

"He'd have come to see you, he said, but you was mad at him for something and he didn't know what."

"I wasn't mad at him," I said. "I figured he was mad at me."

"What was it about?"

I felt ashamed. "It wasn't nothing," I said. "How long is he going to be in New York?"

"I don't know," Horace said. "He said he might get a chance to come around this afternoon."

"Tell him to wait for me. I'll come to see him."

"The cooks ain't going to let you off," Horace said.

"Tell him I'll be there."

What if the cooks didn't want to let me off? I was

139

free, wasn't I? Dinged if I was going to miss the chance to see Dan. For I was determined to tell him I was Willy's sister, and him and me was cousins. I was curious to see if it made any difference to him. I spent the morning being good as pie, peeling potatoes and washing pans, and not sassing anybody and keeping my mouth shut in general, so's nobody would take notice of me, until the second cook asked if I was sick. Then, along about the middle of the afternoon the first cook went to see about fish for supper, and as soon as she was gone the second cook said her old auntie was ailing once again and went off to see her. The third cook fixed herself a glass of rum and water and set down to rest. I picked up the water bucket and went out to the pump with it; and the minute the door closed behind me I skidded off for the President's mansion.

It didn't take but two minutes to get there. Horace was out front gleaming the windows, and looking sour —back at the tavern he'd been a waiter and didn't have to gleam windows.

"Did Dan come yet?"

"He came and went," Horace said. "I told him you was coming, but he was in an all-fired rush. He said he was going down to Columbia College to see Dr. Johnson and get him to sell his notes. He said he didn't dare wait no more. He was afraid the price would go down and they wouldn't be worth nothing."

I was too late. Oh, I kicked myself for not skidding off earlier, and never mind the cooks. "Did he say what he was going to do with the money when he'd sold them?"

"He didn't say. Buy himself free, I reckon, if they come to enough money."

"He's going to buy his Ma free," I said. I didn't dare say that Dan was going to run off after that.

"His Ma? He ain't going to buy himself free?"

"No—" I started to say, when two men come down the street, dressed mighty fine, heading for the President's mansion. I snatched up one of Horace's rags and begun gleaming the windows alongside of him. The two men come up and stopped by the front door. I recognized them right away, Thomas Jefferson and Alexander Hamilton, the tall and the short of the United States government.

I looked at Horace, and he looked at me, and naturally we shut up and concentrated on our gleaming, so as to look like we was working as hard as we could. But I was curious as could be to hear what people like them sounded like, and what they talked about. They was as good as kings and dukes to us.

They stood there by the steps, palavering. I figured they was talking over something they didn't want nobody to hear, which was why they didn't go inside. They didn't pay no attention to me or Horace—we was just niggers to them and part of the furniture, more or less. So we listened.

"Mr. Jefferson, surely you can persuade some of your southern friends in Congress to vote to have the United

141

States pay the states' notes," Mr. Hamilton said. He come up to Mr. Jefferson's chin and had to tip his head back to talk to him.

Mr. Jefferson shook his head. "They take the position that Virginia has paid off most of her notes, and it would be taxing Virginians to put money in the pockets of New Englanders and New Yorkers."

That perked up my curiosity even more: they was talking about them famous notes. I gave Horace a look. He gave me a tiny nod back, and we went on gleaming.

"I can understand their feeling in the matter," Mr. Hamilton said. "It *would* seem unfair. But on the other hand, if we disown the notes entirely and leave them valueless, there'll be tremendous unrest in the north. It could jeopardize the union, I'm confident of that."

"You're probably right," Mr. Jefferson said. "There must be a way around it."

They stopped there at the bottom of the steps. Mr. Hamilton was walking back and forth, excited like, and Mr. Jefferson was holding his chin and staring down at the ground. Then Mr. Hamilton said, "As you know, it seems likely that the government will be moving to Philadelphia, at least temporarily. Perhaps I could persuade my people to see that it moves from there to Virginia. If I did that, do you think you could persuade the Virginia congressmen to vote for paying off all the notes in full?"

That sent a shock right through me, and I come near to dropping the rag. But I hung on and went on gleaming and listening.

142

Mr. Jefferson rubbed his chin again. "It's an interesting idea, but of course the decision is up to Congress. Madison is the key man there. I'll see if I can bring him to see it this way."

Mr. Hamilton smiled. "If you support it, I'm sure it'll go through." He paused. "We have a bargain, then?"

Mr. Jefferson smiled, too. "I'll ask Madison to discuss it with you."

They shook hands, and as they was about to go up the steps, Mr. Hamilton threw us a look. Horace and I caught it in time and was gleaming away. He didn't say nothing, and they went up the steps and into the President's mansion.

Well, I was fired up, all right. I quit pretending I was gleaming anything and flung down the rag. "What was it, Horace?"

"Blame me if it didn't sound like they was making a deal to pay off the notes."

"It seemed like it, for sure. They was making a deal."

Horace nodded. "They was swapping around, that was plain. If Mr. Hamilton would push his side to vote for moving the government south, Mr. Jefferson would push his side to vote for paying off the notes. It's just plain too bad that Dan didn't wait about selling his notes."

"But maybe it ain't too late," I cried. "Maybe he ain't sold them yet, Horace."

And I turned and run just as hard as ever I could up Greenwich Street, to Barkley until I come to the college, a big lawn there, with great trees on it, and then the college, a big stone building three stories high.

Standing out front on the steps was Dan, talking to Dr. Johnson.

I come running up. They give me a look, but I dassn't just burst in, so I stood there and waited for my chance.

"Are you sure, Dan?" Dr. Johnson said.

"Yes, sir," he said. "I don't want to chance it anymore. I want to make sure one of us gets free."

"And you mean to buy your mother's freedom, and not your own?"

"Yes, sir," he said. "It wouldn't be right the other way."

"You might buy your own freedom and then work to save enough to buy your mother as well."

"I thought about that," Dan said. "I calculated it up, and I reckoned it would take so long to save that much she'd probably be dead by then. A black man can't make near as much as a white man."

"That's true," Dr. Johnson said. "But still, it seems to me better to save a young life than an old one. You never can tell what might happen."

"Sir, I've made up—"

I couldn't stand it no longer and I burst in. "Sir, they going to pay off the notes. Mr. Jefferson and Mr. Hamilton, they just agreed."

Well, they looked at me like I was a lunatic. They couldn't say nothing, neither of them, for a minute. Then Dr. Johnson said, "Where on earth did you hear that wild story, Carrie?"

144

So I told them all about it. And when I got done, Dr. Johnson, he questioned me up and down: was I sure it was Mr. Jefferson and Mr. Hamilton, and what did they look like, and was I sure it was the notes they was talking about, and exactly what they said. And finally he was satisfied. He said, "Dan, this all may be true, and it may not. It may just have been a casual conversation of no significance, but my advice is to wait a little while before you sell."

Well, Dan, he could see that, and he said he would wait, and Dan and I walked back to the President's mansion. It didn't make no difference to me at all that he was my cousin. I still loved him just the same. "Dan, was you mad at me for running off crying like that the other time?"

"No, I wasn't mad at you. I thought you were mad at me, but I couldn't figure out why."

"It wasn't nothing," I said. "But I didn't want you to be mad at me. Because I'm going to be your cousin."

Well, he stopped dead on the sidewalk and stared at me. "My cousin?"

"I figured it out, finally," I said. And I told him the whole story—about Colonel Ledyard and the paper Jack Arabus had and such and he stood there looking funnier and funnier, and finally I said, "What's the matter, Dan?"

"Why, I knew Willy had a little sister all along."

"You did?"

"My Ma told me when she figured I was old enough to keep quiet about it. My aunt told her in secret. That

145

was Willy's mother. She told her she had had a little baby when she was captured by the British."

"That was me," I said, sticking my finger in my chest. "Why didn't you tell me?"

"It was a secret. I wasn't supposed to say anything to anybody. How was I to know it was you?"

"What was so secret about it?" I asked.

"Why, Carrie, just think for a minute. Suppose Captain Ivers knew Willy had a sister. He was after Willy, and he'd be after the sister in a minute. He'd say that if Willy was his slave, the sister must be, too. So we was supposed to keep it quiet so he wouldn't find out. We wasn't supposed to take a chance on telling anybody."

"That's why Captain Ivers is after me, then," I said. "He found out somehow. He knows I'm Willy's sister."

Dan thought about it. "I reckon so," he said finally.

"Maybe Willy slipped and said something in front of him," I said.

Dan shook his head. "No, Willy didn't know, either. My Ma didn't dare tell her at first, for fear she *would* slip, and she ain't been back home now for years."

"Then how did Captain Ivers find out?"

Dan shook his head again. "I don't guess we'll ever know," he said. "But I bet he's got those papers Dr. Johnson drew up for my Pa."

But it didn't matter to me. I knew who I was now, clear enough. "I'm free," I said.

Dan touched my arm and we stopped walking along, and looked at each other. "Carrie," he said, "I don't reckon you'd better get your hopes too high. There isn't any way you can prove anything. I believe you're Willy's sister, and I guess Willy will believe it, and my Ma, too, and Mr. Fraunces, and maybe Horace someday. But you can't prove it in court. If Captain Ivers catches you, it'll be his word against yours, and no judge is going to take the word of a nigger kitchen maid over a white man, especially a white man that's got his own ship and money, too."

It shocked me to think that. "But the paper—maybe I can get that paper your Pa had from the British."

Dan shook his head. "We'll probably never get it. And even if we did, it wouldn't do you any good. It doesn't say that you're that little child. The whole thing is just a story. If the white folks don't want to believe it, they won't. Now you're in the same spot Willy is—free, but you can't prove it."

"It isn't fair, Dan," I cried. "It isn't fair."

"No," Dan said, "I reckon it isn't. But Captain Ivers, even he's got to die sometime." Dan looked down at me and I could feel those dinged tears start. He wrapped his arms around my shoulders and hugged me real tight.

"Listen, Carrie, we're kin now. I'm going to watch out for you real good. You and Willy are the only cousins I've got."

It felt good to be hugged like that—even by a cousin. But I couldn't stop the tears, and I couldn't think of nothing to say but just over and over, "It isn't fair, Dan. It isn't fair."

# Epilogue

WHAT FINALLY HAPPENED to Carrie? Did she ever get free? That is a hard question to answer. We know, of course, that in *Jump Ship to Freedom* Dan did buy freedom for his mother and himself. The deal that Alexander Hamilton and Thomas Jefferson worked out on the steps of the President's mansion comes straight from the history books. The southern states agreed to vote in favor of paying off the government notes, which so many Americans held, at full value.

In exchange, the northern states agreed to move the capital city of the new country to the South, where it now is.

Horace, too, got his wish. As part of the deal the capital was moved temporarily to Philadelphia, while the new city that we know today as Washington, D.C., was being built. In August 1790, President Washington left New York for Philadelphia, and of course he would have taken Horace with him. We can presume that Horace finally persuaded Willy to marry him.

Dan, in the end, moved into a little cabin in Connecticut, and began hiring himself out as a sailor to other captains for good wages. He planned to save his money, buy a fishing dory, and go into business for himself.

That still leaves Carrie.

We should remember that at the time of this story, even though there was a lot of feeling in the North and in many southern states, for abolishing slavery, it still went on. Not everybody favored stopping it: people who owned slaves sometimes felt that they would be cheated out of a lot of money if the slaves, whom they had paid good money for, were set free by law. Nonetheless, many people (in the North, anyway) were for freeing the slaves. And in 1785 New York voted against letting slaves be brought into the state to be sold. In 1788 more laws were passed making it easier for blacks to sue whites for their freedom. In 1799 New York voted that all male slaves born after July 4 of that year would be freed when they were twenty-eight, and all females would be freed when they were twenty-five; and by 1810 only a tiny fraction of the blacks in New York and New Jersey were in slavery. Finally, in 1827 New York outlawed slavery altogether.

None of these laws would have helped Carrie until she was much older. The law of 1788 would have made it easier for her to try to prove in court who she was, and of course the 1827 law would have set her free, but she would have been in her forties then. There are other possibilities. She could have run away, most probably to Massachusetts, where slavery was no longer legally supported after 1785. Or she might have run away to Pennsylvania, where Willy and Horace could look after her until she got herself settled. Knowing Carrie, we suspect that she might have done something like that.

But she might not have. The painful fact must be faced that in the eighteenth century it was not easy for blacks to escape from slavery. And it did not always matter if they were born free, as Carrie was, or set free by a master, as Willy was. Blacks in New York and elsewhere were kidnapped off the streets, and once they were enslaved, it was difficult to prove that they were legally free. And it is therefore possible that Captain Ivers finally caught Carrie and sold her off into bondage on a plantation in the South.

Let us hope not, however. Let us hope that she came to a better ending.

# How Much of
# This Book Is True?

FINDING OUT THE TRUTH about things that happened long ago is always difficult. But professional historians have ways of digging out the clues, and putting together a likely picture of the past. Of course, they read important documents, like government records, but they also comb through old newspapers, diaries, letters of people both famous and unknown, gravestones, church records, and many other sources. Thus, although we cannot be sure that we know every detail, it is frequently possible to get a good general picture of how things were at a given time.

The story in this book is, of course, made up. Carrie, Horace, Dan, Willy, and some of the others are our inventions. But the events in which the story is set happened just the way we have them, to the best of our knowledge. Descriptions of Washington's arrival in New York, the inauguration, the President's mansion, the waterfront where Carrie got into so much trouble, and the general details of the city of New York are taken from firsthand accounts given by people who were there at the time. The President did move as we have said, from Cherry Street to Broad Way, and finally to Philadelphia. Mr. Fraunces was indeed his steward, was fired for extravagance and replaced by the Hydes, and then hired back again after the government moved to Philadelphia. Alexander Hamilton, who was the first secretary of the treasury, and Thomas Jefferson, who was the first secretary of state, were as we have drawn them, and they had just the conversation, on the President's steps, that we have reported in this book. The great controversy over the notes was also true, and was settled as part of the compromise worked out by Hamilton and Jefferson in that famous conversation.

Jack Arabus, Dan's father, was also a real person, who won an important case for his freedom against Captain Ivers, who was also real. However, we do not know what kind of person Captain Ivers was: he probably was not so evil a person as we have made him out to be. (We have told the story of Ivers and Arabus in another book, *War Comes to Willy Freeman*.)

In one way our stories about Willy and Dan and Carrie do not fit the historical truth. Only a very small proportion of American slaves received their freedom before the Civil War, which took place seventy years after this story ends. The majority of slaves lived out their lives on southern plantations working hard and in constant threat of being sold away from their families. The lives of Willy and Dan are more representative of blacks in the North, but even there few slaves gained their freedom in the eighteenth century, although northern states gradually ended slavery. Carrie, who may never have gained her freedom, is probably the most typical case.

Samuel Fraunces is a particularly interesting character. He was generally called "Black Sam" Fraunces during his lifetime, and it has been assumed by some historians that he was a black. However, our research indicates that he was in fact considered white, despite the nickname. At that time, and indeed at other times, too, a dark-complected person or even one with black hair, might be nicknamed "Black" no matter what his race. In any case, his taverns were considered the finest in New York, and were the site of many important events, including Washington's famous farewell address to his officers at the end of the Revolution. Fraunces Tavern still exists on the site of the old tavern on Pearl Street in New York City. The original building burned down many years ago and nobody is exactly sure what it looked like, but the present building is an attempt to reproduce what it might have looked like. There is a museum upstairs that contains many pictures, maps, furniture, tableware, and other relics from that time.

A word about the language used in this book: We know how people in those days wrote because we have

157

many examples of their letters and diaries. We do not, however, know how they spoke, because the words have long since melted in the air. However, they almost certainly did not speak the way we have given it in this book. What we have tried to do here is to give the "feel" of the speech of an illiterate slave of the times, in such a way as to be comprehensible to modern readers. It should not be taken as being historically accurate.

In particular, we had to consider very carefully our use of the word *nigger*. The term is offensive to modern readers, and we certainly do not intend to be insulting. But it was commonly used in America right into the twentieth century, and it would have been a distortion of history to avoid its use entirely.

But language aside, we have tried to be as accurate as we possibly could about the details of life as it was lived in New York City at the end of the eighteenth century. We have studied tavern menus for the things people ate and drank, advertisements for how they dressed, newspaper reports for what they did for entertainment. It is true, for example, that the President took a party of people, including William Samuel Johnson, out to the theater during the Christmas season, as we mention. In sum, we have tried to give readers a sense of how it was to live in those times—what people said, did, thought, and felt.

# About the Authors

# About the Authors

**James Lincoln Collier** is the coauthor, with his brother Christopher Collier, of the Newbery Honor Book *My Brother Sam Is Dead*, *The Bloody Country*, *The Winter Hero*, *War Comes to Willy Freeman*, and *Jump Ship to Freedom*. He has written many other highly acclaimed books for young readers, including *The Teddy Bear Habit* and, for adults, *The Making of Jazz* and *Louis Armstrong: An American Genius*. He lives in New York City.

**Christopher Collier** is a professor of history at the University of Bridgeport in Connecticut. His field is early American history, especially the American Revolution. He is the author of *Roger Sherman's Connecticut: Yankee Politics and the American Revolution* and other works. He and his family live in Orange, Connecticut.